To,
Tom

# FISHERMAN'S BLUES

*Best wishes*
*Mick Donnellan*

*A Novel*

*By*

## Mick Donnellan

ORIGINAL WRITING

ISBNS
PARENT : 978-1-78237-764-1
EPUB: 978-1-78237-765-8
MOBI: 978-1-78237-766-5
PDF: 978-1-78237-767-2

A CIP catalogue for this book is available from the National Library.

Published by ORIGINAL WRITING LTD., Dublin, 2014.

Printed by CLONDALKIN GROUP, Glasnevin, Dublin 11

# ACKNOWLEDGEMENTS

Special thanks to

Noreen Lydon for providing the original Cover Artwork.


The author acknowledges the support of

Ballinrobe Credit Union.

*For Michelle and Nairobi.*

*Jack.*

*The waitress is practicing politics.*

Shtop, cuntish. The dole cut me off. Like that. Went to the bank and the Pass Machine said: **Insufficient Funds.**

There was the money: Gone.

Prayed it was a glitch. Went to the Social Welfare. They kinda cringed when they saw me coming. Fella behind the counter opened with: 'Howya, Jack.'

'Not great,' I said. 'My dole money didn't go through.'

'You're on it a while now.'

'That's right,' I said. 'A valued customer.'

He did the thing with the eyebrows, went: 'I don't know about that. Way things are you see....have you got your PPS card with you there...?'

I took it out and gave it to him. He swiped it through. Frowned at what came up. Tapped his pencil on the table and asked: 'No sign of work at all, Jack?'

'No.'

'Hmm...new rules in you see...'

'What are they?'

'You'll have to get a job.'

'*Have* to?'

'You're signing for the last ten years.'

'But there's no work.'

'Have ya tried JOBbridge?'

'Heh?'

—

Later at the JOBbridge office.

What are my qualifications?

I didn't have any.

What kinda work am I prepared to do?

Nothin.

How did I feel about Galway?

Not great.

Things got awkward. There was a telesales job going, they said. Starting Monday. "...Sure try it and see how you get on...."

—

The bus cost €12.80. The office was on Merchant Road. The red painted door contrasted with the grey buildings around it. Written across the top was:

Fortune Travel
*Where dreams come true.*

Inside, it smelled like the warm paper from a photocopier. The lights were bright and the walls a dark shade of ocean blue. I was looking for a supervisor called Chris. Found him. He shook my hand and showed me the ropes. There was a list of names and numbers, photocopied from the phonebook. He described them as *Leads*. Go down through them, he said. Do your best.

But what am I sellin?

'Nothin. You're makin appointments. We're an investment company for buyers of foreign property. We want people to come to our seminar in a hotel by the docks. There's a crew down there that'll take care of the sellin. You just make sure the leads turn up...'

The cubicles were all lined in rows, like a classroom. I looked around at everyone else. Some young. Some old. Some of them standing up, talking at high speed. Using their hands to make a point, like they were conducting an orchestra. Chris went on. '...we all get a computer and a headset. Our targets are ten appointments a night or *not less* than forty-six a week. You go below that and you're fired. It's that simple. Each hit brings €20 commission and anythin after *fifty* hits counts as a bonus.' He handed me the leads. 'Get crackin.'

Get crackin? Shtop. I sat down. Felt shaky, up against it. Pressure.

He gave me a script with all the right things to say. It's supposed to be what they want to hear. I put on the headset and went LIVE. My first call came through like a voice from the beyond. The screen was flashing with:

Martin Cleary,
Bog Road,
Ballyhaunis.

I went for: 'Hello, Mr. Cleary?'
'Yeah?'
'Jack here, from *Fortune Travel*, in Galway. It's just a…'
'What the fuck do you want?'
'We're offerin…'
'I don't want it.'
'Well…'
'Fuck off. Get a real job.'
He hung up. Beep. The next lead is:

**Mary-Anne Rochford,**
**Bellmullet.**
**Co. Mayo.**

'Hello, this is Jack here from *Fortune Travel* in Galway. How are you this evenin?'
'I'm very well, thank you. How can I help you, Jack?'
Thought: Not too bad. Went: 'Well, we see that you filled out a questionnaire for us recently?'
She changed tone then. No more Queen Elizabeth. 'Is this a sales call?'
'No, not at all.'
'It is, isn't it?'
'No, if you'd just let me explain…'
'You're one of those…time-share…pyramid scheme people, aren't you?'
'No, Mrs. Rochford. We're just offerin…'
'I *knew* it. Let me put you on to my husband.'

'Hang on.'

A gruff voice says: 'Hello?'

'Hello, sir. This is Jack from...'

'I don't care.'

'We're givin away free weekends in a Galway hotel.'

'Shove it up your hole.'

He hung up. Mighty start. I looked at my watch. Another two hours before the bus went. Decided to go for a sneaky pint. Waited for Chris to turn his back and I slipped away out the door.

First time in Galway since Christmas. Serious spot. Kicked stones up Shop Street. The air was cool but not cold. Outside Corbett Court, a busker sang *Piano Man*, by *Billy Joel*.

Inside *McSwiggan's*. There was a couple of yuppies at the counter, talking about contract phones and low rate credit cards. A girl sat to the right on her own, painted nails, red coat, plastic face, smatherin with text messages. *U2* played *Pride (in the name of love)*. The back bar was empty so I pulled up a stool and ordered a *Guinness* from a waitress called Stella. She was the best looking woman I'd seen in a long time. Long brown hair and a hundred watt smile. How am I doing this evening?

'Better now. Just waitin for the bus.'

She smiled. I fell in love. She said: 'Nice shirt.'

'Bought it this mornin. €7 in a sale.'

She didn't answer. Just left the pint on the counter and went out the back with her catwalk curves.

Bono was now singing: *With or without you.*

Aragh fuck Bono.

I sank the pint til there was nothing left except that frothy bit at the bottom. Tapped the counter to make Stella come back so I could order another. She was confused but got it anyway.

Took my time with this one. Let the stomach settle. After, I hit the Brandy &Baileys. It tasted like your favourite ice cream. Drank four and lost count. Stella was getting worried, like we were trapped in a lift and I was jumping up and down. My phone rang. It was the JOBbridge office. 'Hello, Jack?'

'How's things?'

'Is that Jack?'

'Are ye well?'

'Jack…is that you?'

'Who are ya lookin for?'

'We're looking for Jack…'

'Yeah. He was here a while ago and ah… now he's gone somewhere.'

Stutter, then: '….ah…any idea…where…this is JOBbridge here and we need to talk to him urgently…?'

I left it a second, like it was bad reception, then said: 'Hello? Hello?' and I hung up.

Stella was watching me with bright blue wary eyes. They were like chandeliers stuck inside her head. I gave her a wink and finished off the fluffy duck. Only twenty Euro left to my name. Dwindling fast. Bought fags. Dwindling faster now. Black night through the windows, delighted rain belting against the glass. I looked at the time and realised the bus was long gone and I'd nowhere to stay and probably no job. Decided to spend my last tenner on a vodka with *Redbull* and hope for the best. Sure maybe even Stella might bring me home? When she got the drink, she left to talk to someone. Calling a taxi no doubt for the two of us.

Took a drunk scan around. Empty now. Everything looked like it was being shot through a shaky camera. Blair Witch job. I reached for the glass, missed it and knocked it over the counter. It fell with a smash and the ice scattered all the way to the front bar. The drink followed, like a stream of runaway piss. I stood up, in a desperate attempt to plead my case with nobody at all. The stool fell behind me and was still clattering when Stella and some prick called John landed out. He'd his arms folded and he was playing it thick. I tried to pretend the stool wasn't happening but it sounded like an artic lorry had crashed into a furniture shop.

We stood looking at each other for a while. I don't know how long. He eventually said: 'That's your last drink.'

I pointed to Stella. 'Thanks be to fuck for that. I thought she was goin to let me go on all night.'

She let fly then, all salty confidence with: 'I think you should leave.'

Knew it was inevitable but still felt hurt. Was searching for an answer when the bouncers caught me. Under the arms. Polite aggression.

Suddenly I'm outside. Issuing all sorts of threats from terrorist associations to vigilantism and arson. Then I'm walking around Woodquay. Half lost, mostly demented. It was raining worse than ever. I took out my phone and the last three numbers were the Chinese in Ballinrobe, JOBbridge, and *Fortune Travel*.

A car breezed by and splashed a load of water against my legs. And then I puked all sorts of colours over the Salmon Weir Bridge. After, I wiped my mouth and pressed: *Dial*.

Pure cuntish entirely.

*Your heroes for ghosts.*

Woke up on a couch. There was a smell of dogs and coffee. Blanket over me. Stomach queasy. Aftertaste of puke. Dynamite going off in the brain. Counter to the right. Sensed someone there. The page of a newspaper turning.

Left it a few seconds.

Let the flashbacks kick in.

Then thought: "Fuck that." And stuck my head up.

It was Chris. He didn't look happy at all. He opened with: 'You're some fuckin eejit.'

'I've been told that before.'

'Two phone calls is all ya lasted.'

'Any chance of a tenner for the bus?'

He grunted in a way that said: *Not a fuckin hope, sunshine.*

I lied back on the couch. There was weird shapes on the ceiling. He left it a few seconds, then said: 'We're on again in an hour.'

'*On* where?'

'Work.'

'Oh no....'

'You've no choice. We need you.'

'Why's that?'

'Cos I said so.'

'Sure just gimme the price of the bus and I'll be out of your way.'

'No can do.'

It went on like that. Him saying there was no choice. Me protesting.

We were back in the office again that afternoon. The air conditioning was set to *cold*. The tables were clean and smelled like lemon. There was a board on the wall with names and how many appointments they'd made. Mine was on the bottom.

I sparked a bottle of *Lucozade* and used my monitor to hide from view.

Spent the time scribbling on the back of the leads and checking out a young one at the end of the row. I was suicidal after twenty minutes.

My mobile rang. It was JOBbridge again. I rejected it. Looked around. Thought about pulling another Houdini but I'd no cash. Contemplated robbing a busker but I'd feel too guilty. Decided to make a few calls. Worst that could happen is I'd make money.

They were all the same as yesterday. Fuck off. Get a job. Don't call again. That kinda thing. A while later, two suits arrived with briefcases. They looked like undertakers. Chris got to attention and made them feel important. They browsed around, listening to us on the phone, keeping an eye on the time. They watched me for a while, said something and left.

After, Chris, came down, said: 'Drinks with the management later. Me and you in *The Living Room*.'

'Huh?'

'Just keep ringin til then.'

My next call had a seductive voice. I started my script and she cut me dead with: 'Let me guess, a pyramid scheme?'

'Why does everyone think that? No. It's not. It's villas in Bulgaria.'

She laughed, sincerely, and said: 'Why not try selling me a piece of the moon?'

'It's not as profitable.'

I heard her take a drag from a cigarette. 'My boyfriend isn't home. Maybe you should be talking to him.'

'When's he back?'

'Later.'

'After six?'

'Maybe.'

'Is he rich?'

'He's got money.'

'Does he like to part with it?'

'No.'

'Treats you well?'

'What's that got to do with anything?'

'I'm curious.'

'He makes me feel safe.'

'You don't sound insecure.'

'We've only been talking thirty seconds.'

'And I still haven't made an appointment.'

She dragged again, said: 'Then you need to try harder.'

'I'll send you an invite to our seminars.'

'Are they a waste of time?'

'Probably if you're not buyin anythin.'

'Then why would I want to go?'

'To meet me.'

'And what then?'

'Love at first sight. Just like the films.'

She laughed again. I looked at the screen. It was Mr. Graham Reynolds. 'All I have is a Graham Reynolds here.'

'That's all you need to know.'

'How will I recognise you?'

'I never said I was coming.'

'But if you do.'

'I'll be the most beautiful.'

Pause. 'I can't think of anythin else to say.'

'I thought it was *your job* to talk?'

'Yeah, but I only started yesterday.'

'Oh.' She said. 'That's a pity.'

And she hung up.

There was a tremor in my hand as I put through the invite.

—

Eight o'clock came and Chris shouted: "Phones down!"

I was delighted and thirsty. Wondering what the management wanted. Maybe they'd fire me. Letting me down gently. Didn't give two fucks as long as *they* bought the pints. The young one at the end of the row was packing up. I made the approach. Casual, like I was just wandering past, asked: 'How's things?

She tutted, Kardashian style, and said: 'I have a boyfriend.'

'Who asked if you've got a boyfriend?'

She rolled her eyes and walked out.

Chris said: 'Never mind that one. She's after gettin fired.'

'How d'ya mean?'

'She was fuckin useless.'

'Worse than me?'

'Shtop. Are ya right?'

'Yeah.'

We pulled down the shutters. The night was vibrant. Flame throwers on Quay Street. Smell of Paraffin. We had a fast one in *Taafe's* where there was trad music and bearded island types swamping *Guinness*. Made our way to *The Living Room* after. The drink was swirling in my stomach but doing great for the fire of thirst inside. I let out a big burp and a hippy doll with braids gave me a dirty look. I shrugged and Chris lit a smoke and gave me the box. I sparked, feeling like big shtuff, and inhaled hard.

We sifted through the crowd, like a large boat going through debris on the water. Same busker sang *Pink Floyd - Wish You Were Here*. The song caught me somewhere in the brain. Brought me somewhere. Chris threw him his change.

There was a light drizzle as we reached *The Living Room*. Two bouncers, earphones and jackets, gave us the nod. One of them pulled back the door and we threw our cigarettes in the drain outside. A fella behind us was turned away for wearing runners.

The place was dim. A smell of fried food and a distant odour of ketchup. A couple ate club sandwiches at a table to the left. A blonde waitress walked passed with a basket of chips. We got two pints of *Carlsberg* and searched around for the undertakers. Found them in an open area at the back, the two of them drinking *Ginger Ale*, looking like they were in casualty. Both about the same age, maybe early forties. One guy had brown hair, the other black, with a tache, looked like Charlie Chaplin. We pressed the flesh. Chaplin said: 'Thanks for comin.'

'No problem.' Silence, I said: 'So, what did ye want to talk about?'

They exchanged looks. Chaplin continued. 'Hasn't Chris told you anythin?'

'No.'

Chris shrugged, said: 'I thought he knew.'

The other guy had a pale face and light blue eyes, looked like Chris Tarrant. He spoke. 'You had the most successful record in your last job as a Company Rep. Now that you're with *us*, we think your talents could be maximised if you were promoted.'

He opened the briefcase, took out some papers and continued. 'We have a contract here. If you sign today, your wages will double, as will your commission, and *we'll* pay your expenses. At the moment, we're recruiting all our best employees in a bid to increase our margins by the end of the year. This is the job we hired you for, we just put you in the office until we got a chance to make it down and chat. We were actually headhunting you for the position when your name appeared on the JOBbridge Database....'

There was something awful wrong here, but I didn't want to fuck it up before they bought a round, asked: 'Mind if I order a pint?'

'Yes of course, *John*. On us.'

The picture was coming together. They thought I was someone else. I'll have another *Carlsberg*, please. Fasht. Hit them with: 'You still haven't told me what the job is.'

Chaplin answered. 'You'll be doin the same thing as you are on the phone. As you know, our customers are awarded a free weekend at our hotel. Our company also has a number of developments abroad and we're currently lookin for investors. When the leads come to stay, we'd like someone competent there to show them their options.'

'And get them to invest?'

'Essentially, yes. We're generous, but we're not a charity. Your number one job will be closin them down, makin the sale before they leave. It's a tough market, and we need the best.'

'And it's all done at the weekends?'

'Yes.'

'What if I say No?'

'Most of our branches are bein downsized, and in some parts closed. There's no guarantee you'll still be employed at that office even one month from now.'

'Sounds too good to be true.'

'It's called success.'

I looked at Chris, he said: 'Up to you.'

The waitress arrived with the *Carlsberg*. I said thanks, then: 'Can I have two more actually. I'm very thirsty.'

There was an awkward silence. Chaplin shifted his arse in the seat. She smiled and went to get it.

I pretended to think for a minute, said 'Ok. I'll do your job, whatever it is.'

'Good.' Said Chaplin. He produced a pen and slid over the contract. 'Just need your John Hancock here.'

Put a scribble that started with *John*. They didn't even look, just threw the whole lot in the briefcase and Tarrant said: 'We'll be in touch soon. Be ready.'

They left. The extra pints came. Chris asked: 'What do ya reckon?'

'On the waitress?'

'No! The fuckin job.'

'Oh yeah.' I took a nervous sip. 'Can't wait.'

He looked at me. Calculating. Then went: 'Why do you go by *Jack*, if your name's *John*?'

'Cos my name's not *John*, Chris. And I haven't a clue what's goin on.'

'Heh?'

'Yeah.'

'Why? What exactly did they tell you in JOBbridge?'

I told him exactly what they told me in JOBbridge and he said: 'Oh sweet fuckin Jesus.'

*Because you intrigue me.*

JOBbridge fucked it up. I wasn't supposed to be here. John Hanover was. Who's John Hanover? Haven't a clue. Some prick with the best Telesales record in the country. Got fired from his last job cos he went to fuck on the sauce. Now *Fortune Travel* think they have him. Through JOBbridge.

'We can't do anythin about it.' Said Chris. 'I'll look like a bollox if I tell them.'

'So I'll just keep goin?'

'Be nice if you made a few appointments, too.'

'I don't even have a place to live.'

'There's a spare room at mine. You can stay there for a while.'

We were back in the office the next day. I was green with drink. The cute one in the top row was gone. I thought that was fairly sad and I told Chris. He told me to be careful, I just about hanging in there myself. I decided to ring the flirty bitch from the night before. Got her name from the directory on the computer. *Reynold's* residence. She answered after two.

I said: 'How's things?'

'Hello?'

'How're ya gettin on?'

'Good, thanks ....and this is...?'

'Jack here. *Fortune Travel.* I rang yesterday.'

'Oh. I said: "No" – *didn't I?*'

'You didn't put it either way, so I'm just doin a sort of a follow up call...'

'Well, this is a bad time. I'm having dinner.'

'What are you having?'

'Food.'

'Why not have dinner on us? We're offerin the finest food and views in the West of Ireland.'

She thought and said: 'I don't think you really want to sell me anything.'

'Then why would I call?'

'Because I intrigue you.'

'Don't be ridiculous. I'm a professional.'

Chris looked up, frowned and went back to his call.

She said: 'And I'm attached.'

'But you sound bored.'

'It's better than miserable.'

'Come for a drink with me, it might be excitin.'

'No.'

'Why not?'

'I'm a faithful girlfriend.'

'Or playin hard to get.'

'Why're you so interested?'

'Because you intrigue me.'

'I intrigue a lot of men. You could be a psycho.'

'We'll go somewhere public. Say *The King's Head* tomorrow night, bout 9?'

'I have go now.'

'I'll be at the bar, by the entrance.'

Click. Chris asked: 'What the hell was that?'

'Lead I had yesterday.'

'You close her?'

'Yeah. How're you doin?'

'Nearly finished. Let's get this shit wrapped up.'

We packed everything away. Set the alarm and pulled down the steel shutter. Turned around and a fella stood waiting. Long trench coat and serious face. Chris looked at him and said: 'Hello?'

He flashed a wallet or something. 'My name is Kurt Jennings. I'm a Private Detective.'

Chris shrugged, said: 'Glad to hear it. What's that got to do with us?'

'We better have a chat.'

'Well, the boss isn't here.'

Silence. He had a silver stubble and watery eyes. His face was cracked and I couldn't see his teeth in the dark, but I guessed they were the colour of cheese. He said: 'A lot of people want their money back.'

'Nothin to do with me. I'm just lockin up for the night.'

'What's your name?'

'None of your business.'

Jennings hadn't looked at me. He said: 'Can I go inside?'

'Only staff are allowed into the buildin. And what the fuck for?'

'How long have you worked here?'

'Long enough.'

'What do you know about the operation in Bulgaria?'

'Will you ever go fuck yourself.'

He took out a pack of smokes. Sweet Afton. No tips. He tapped one on the box and sparked, said: 'D'you know a fella called Frank Rowland?'

'What if I do?'

He took a drag, some tobacco stuck on his lip. Cars breezed past behind him. I felt like I should say something. Nothing came. Jennings looked at me, asked: 'Who are you?'

Chris answered. 'Employee. Doin overtime.'

Jennings turned back. 'Let him answer.'

I said: 'What's it matter who *I* am?'

'Nothin to me, buddy. I'm just doin my job for the people ye all fucked out of money.'

Chris said: 'We have to go.'

Jennings pulled on his smoke. 'See ye round, lads.'

Could feel him watching us as we walked. Out of earshot, I said: 'I didn't know fellas like him existed.'

'He looks like a wino.'

'Who's Frank Rowland?'

'The fella behind the company. Never met him, but heard he's a bit wild.'

'Wild?'

'But that's not what he's after.'

'How d'ya mean?'

'He probably knows you're new and thinks he can squeeze you somehow...'

'How would he know that?'

'There's cunts everywhere watchin.'

'And what could I tell him? Who's gettin fucked outta money?'

'Dunno. He's probably ravin…but you hear stories sometimes about how what we do is a bit….dodgy.'

We turned a corner. It was starting to rain. I said: 'What'll we do now?'

'Pint?'

'Yeah, fuck it.'

*What if all these fantasies come flailing around....*

Next night in *The King's Head*. I was early. Ordered a *Carlsberg* and watched a match on the big screen. Liverpool and Arsenal. The gunners were down a goal. I was feeling bulletproof. Wondered why I didn't move up to Galway a lot sooner. Ten years in Ballinrobe on the piss. Doing nothing. Drawing the dole. A working class hero with no work and no heroics.

There was movement beside me. I turned round, expecting your one from the phone. It was Jennings. I stayed composed. He smelled like a wet dead crow. Still had the grey stubble and his hair was polished and greasy. I was surprised he'd made it through the bouncers. I said: 'I was waitin for someone a lot better lookin than you....what the fuck d'ya want?'

*Phil Collins* came on in the background with *Another Day in Paradise*. He said: 'What do you think of Phil?'

'He's ok, but that doesn't answer my question.'

He ordered a *Blackbush* and water, asked: 'Were ye sellin paradise today?'

'Wha?

'Ye're a crowd of fuckin scumbags, d'ye know that?'

'So?'

'How long do ye think you can get away with it?'

'With what?'

He took a drink with a shaking hand and said: 'You don't even know what you're involved in, do ya?'

'No. But I'm gettin paid well.'

'You took a job meant for someone else.'

'So?'

'So you're not John Hanover.' The smell of him got worse. It was like sour milk, emanating from a bag of turf. 'Are you waitin for someone you care about?'

'I don't know yet.'

He sort of laughed. Nice and bitter like. Sneering at the same time. You know these type of pricks? Then he goes: 'You're fucked so.'

He threw back the rest of his drink and left. I shrugged and turned to the television. Someone had switched to the news and the headlines were all about the economy. When I turned back around, she was there. Emerald eyes and pale face. All black attire, looked good. Short skirt and high black boots. Dark hair and a face the shape of a heart. Smooth legs. Somehow, I knew she'd look like this. I played calm, said: 'You must be Miss Reynolds?'

Her voice was soft, like warm strawberry milk. 'Dyane, actually.'

'Drink?'

'What do you think?'

She had a *Martini*, I said: 'Fancy juice?'

She rolled her eyes, said: 'Whatever.'

We got talking. I asked: 'So, is this your first date with adultery?'

'Nothing's happened. We're just talking. But I'm not in the business of meeting strange men in bars.'

'How's it feel?'

'Like I'm at the airport, waiting for a plane to a faraway place.'

She sipped the *Martini* with delicate, polished hands. Silver rings and a bracelet.

'Where's Graham tonight?'

'Playing Poker.'

'Did you convince him to come to the seminar?'

'No. Do those villas even exist?'

'I'm not even sure.'

'I knew you were a chancer the second I picked up the phone.'

An hour flew by.

Most important point was: Her life lacked passion.

In her job.

In her mind.

In the bedroom.

She asked: 'Do you have something planned for the night, or are you just winging it?'

'Wingin it. D'you want to come back to mine?'

'Don't be so pushy.'

'I could be passionate.'

'You're an awful shaper.'

'Maybe that's why you're attracted to me.'

'I want a cigarette. And another *Martini* when I get back.'

She walked out. Slow and confident. I tapped the counter and looked around. Quiet buzz, pints going down well. Thought about Jennings. Fuck him. Few minutes later, she came back, whiff of tobacco, said: 'How come you don't have a girlfriend?'

'Maybe I do.'

'Really?'

'No. Not really lookin either.'

'So, you just want to fuck me and disappear?'

'It sounds weird when you curse. You're so polished besides.'

'Don't change the subject.'

'You do more than intrigue me. I don't know why, but I like you.'

'Is that supposed to be a compliment?'

'I'm just bein honest.'

'You hardly even know me.'

'Seriously, are you happy?'

'I hate when people ask me that.'

Night going well. I wished it was over before I had time to fuck it up. A pause came and she asked: 'Do you want to walk me home?'

Walking, we held hands. Came around by Dominic Street and went towards Father Griffin road. The busker was singing REM *Losing my Religion*.

Light rain, stars. She said: 'I like you too, Jack.'

'I'm glad.'

'But you're kind of different.'

'I think it excites you.'

'It does. But I'm not used to it.'

'All the better.'

'I don't think this would work. I just feel like there's too much at stake. I love Graham.'

'You don't sound convinced.'

'In a weird way, I do.'

Gave her my number, said: 'Sure give me a shout some time.'

She stood on her toes, kissed me on the cheek and said: 'Thank you.'

And I watched her til she turned the corner.

*Marylyn, my bitterness.*

A week passed. Chris got the call to close down the office. Myself and himself were to start at the hotel straight away. Tarrant said to: "Fire everyone else."

Some of them protested and Chris promised to do all he could. Soon's they were gone he went: "Fuck them."

Chaplin met us at the door the next day, said: 'Fair play to ye.'

Chris asked: 'So, what now?'

'The presentation's not for an hour yet, but come in and meet everyone else.'

We walked through the foyer and took a right. The place was plush. Leather suites and a fake fire. Lotsa flowers and women in mango uniforms. Cream walls with bad paintings. Everything smelled like crayon.

*The Cruxshadows - Marilyn, My Bitterness*, rode with me.

In the conference room. Bright place with chandeliers and tall red curtains. Some jugs of lemon water on a counter by the wall. Our team sat near the top, by the stage, chatting loudly. They were all suits and confidence and under thirty.

Chaplin got everyone's attention with: 'Ok folks, everyone's here, enough of the talkin shite. You all know the story. We give our customers a free weekend in the hotel on the condition that they come to our seminar today and consider our deals on Bulgarian property. *Your* job will be to sell it to them. If ye don't want to sell, you get the fuck out. If ye don't like pressure, you get the fuck out. If ye don't want to be rich, then stop wastin my time and fuck off home. Ye're all here because ye're the best at what ye do. It's why ye're gettin the best money in the business. Today, we have over a hundred people comin through them doors. They're all stayin here in the hotel, upstairs, at our considerable expense, but every one of them has ten thousand they're willin to invest. They don't know it yet, but they do, and *ye're* goin to convince them.' He let that settle, then raised his voice with: 'I don't want to hear shite about tough customers. I don't want to hear about people gettin up and walkin out without leavin any cash. If I do, then ye're goin with them. Everyone has to be closed today. And that means *everyone*.' He looked at his watch and went on. 'Ok, it's ten o'clock. The first talk is at eleven. I want you all outside, gettin to know them as they come in, makin them feel comfortable. I want them all buttered up and feelin like they're in on the best deal of their lives. Then I'm goin to show them the stuff inside, hand out some wine and tell them you've been sellin all mornin. When they land out here, you need to look frantic. Ok? Look like you've been wheelin and dealin. You're busy people. Deals are happenin. Property's gettin snapped up. They need to buy *now* or forget about it.'

No women on the team. All lads with arms folded and ready to *close the deal*. He went on to explain how we take the money – debit and credit cards, cheques, or a combination of both. Cash too if they had it. He brought us around in a circle. Showed us the contract and where the customers were supposed to sign. Each of us got a desk, a phone and an EFT reader. We were also given a briefcase full of contracts and brochures about Bulgaria and then they assigned us to different rooms around the hotel.

Outside in the lobby, the leads were starting to arrive from upstairs. All starry eyed and looking amazed. They walked off the lifts and stood around, drinking bad tea and eating biscuits. There was conversations about babysitters, the need for a holiday, being lucky. I stopped and talked to a few. Gave them my name and welcomed them to the hotel. After a while, Chaplin invited everyone to sit down for the presentation.

They all got seated and I sat at the back. I was curious to see him in action. He was at the front, fiddling with a laptop. On the wall behind him was a projected picture of the Bulgarian coastline. The crowd were all chatter and the waiters walked around offering expensive wine. There was a banner across the top of the stage that said:

Fortune Travel.
*Sharing the Wealth.*

Chaplin hooked a mini-microphone to his jacket. He turned a button at the side. There was a slight screech of feedback. This got everyone's attention. They all looked towards him. He opened. 'Hello, can everybody hear me?'

They muttered. He spoke louder. 'Can EVERYBODY hear me?'

'Yes.' They said in unison.

He had the posh accent going full blast.

'Good. I'd like to start by welcoming you all here today. Some of you may have had plans this weekend, but you'll be glad you cancelled. My name is Jim Brown and I'm a very successful investor in foreign property.'

He hit a button on the laptop. 'How many of you have ever dreamed of owning your own villa? Do you think it's something for the millionaires and billionaires? An indulgence that you just *can't* afford?' They all seemed to agree. He smiled and said: 'Let's shatter that myth...'

He kicked off. Showed them pictures of investors from the past. Men that lost their jobs and took a gamble with the redundancy. Now they're loaded. People sitting on yachts in the Caribbean. Chaplin pressing the flesh with the Bulgarian politicians (Photoshop job). He was like a mesmerist or a religious preacher, had them all hooked. You could see the daydream behind their eyes. He kept it nice and short too, just under an hour, let them get excited, then closed up when he felt the room was buzzing: 'Ok, that's the end of the presentation. I'd like you all to digest what you've heard and, if still interested, our representatives are here to answer all your questions and take a deposit. Please be patient, as demand is very high. We try to accommodate everyone, but be decisive. If you *are* interested, then let us know *now*. Time is money and the profits are waiting. Today, you can decide to take positive control of your financial future. All you need is one word: YES. Thank you.'

The crowd clapped loudly, like they really meant it. So I went out to the lobby and waited. Half convinced to buy one myself.

## *Just as long as they'll definitely be built, like?*

They all landed out. Wondering want to do next. I met Chris walking down the corridor. He was carrying a small table. 'For the office. Go get yours.'

Walked up and Chaplin was waiting. He pointed at a desk with a briefcase on top. 'Take these and come back for the rest.'

Picked it up and followed Chris. The room was spacious and warm. Light green carpet and blue walls. There was a box of brochures in the corner. I picked one up and it smelled of fresh ink, like the first day at school. There was a picture of a couple on the front. They both looked like models. There was a quote beside them saying *"Fortune Travel changed my life!"*

'Story is,' Said Chris. 'We invite them down here and give them a seat. Take out all the brochures and shit and make them nervous. We need to put them under serious pressure. Force them into a position of choice. Act like all the apartments, or villas, or whatever the fuck, are nearly bought up and this is their last chance café. If they don't buy now, they miss the bus and they don't get rich. If you want to give them a minute to think, pretend you have to go outside and speak to some other interested clients. We never leave the room at the same time because they'll have a chance to talk to the other couples and express doubts. Keep it focused on *them*, make them think it's all about makin the right decision. Then make your *close*.'

'Just you and me in here?'

'Yeah. Two in each room.'

'And when do they get to see the properties?'

'They don't.'

'*They don't?*'

'No.'

'Why?'

'Cos the fuckin things don't even exist.'

'Heh?!'

'Yeah, it's all a scam. Figure that.'

'Fuck.'

—

My first couple were young. Late twenties. Chaplin opened the door and said at the same time. 'Our man here will take care of you inside...'

They wandered in and I sat behind the desk.

'Hello, folks, my name is Jack. I'm an agent with the company here today.'

They both checked me out. I was in a new suit. Bought for the new job. A real yuppie uniform. They looked at each other. The guy said: 'Jack, howya doin? I'm Robert and this is Auburn.'

He was in a plaid shirt and fancy jacket, jeans and brown shoes. Bright blue eyes and hair slightly greying at the sides. I shook his hand. It was warm and strong, like he wanted to do business. 'Robert, nice to meet you.' Pause. 'Did you both like the presentation?'

Auburn was in first: 'I thought it was great, wasn't it, Rob?'

She was in a long black dress that reached her ankles. Tight around the hips. Light white shirt, big chest and a golden necklace. Brown curly hair and eyes like hazelnuts.

Rob said: 'Yeah, it was now in fairness. I didn't know it was so easy to buy property abroad. Twenty grand sure is nothin for a place like that.'

Decided to open up the shite talk factory. All the one at this stage. 'That's what all the smart people are sayin anyway, Rob.'

'And c'mere to me. Do ye do all the paperwork and all that?'

'We do.'

Auburn asked: 'And does that cost more?'

'No. Twenty grand covers the lot. Ten now and ten when they're built....'

Rob said: 'I heard bad stories about this kinda thing before, though...'

'Sure didn't we all, Rob? But this is legit all the way. We have VAT Codes and Registered Numbers and anythin else you might want. It's simply that the market has finally hit "Rock Bottom." Remember everyone before sayin: "Why didn't we buy *early*?"'

'I was onea them!' Said Rob.

'Well Bulgaria is the new early. As early as it gets.'

Auburn said: 'Just as long as they'll definitely be built, like?'

'Oh they will….'

'For sure?' She said. 'How can we know, like?'

'You can go and visit our sister company out there.'

'Really?'

'Any time you like. Work it into your holiday.' Went for the pure shlurry altogether with: 'I was there myself last month.'

Auburn said: 'Oh, do you have an apartment out there, too?'

'I do.'

'You'd recommend it so?' Said Rob.

'I would.'

'No problems?'

'Not a one. Simpler than Ireland to buy a place, and better weather too.'

They laughed at that. Rob said: 'We're just back from honeymoon.'

'Oh, how'd that go?'

'Great. Malta.'

'Nice?'

'Mighty. Time for reality now, though. But this might be a good start for the next holiday.'

'Twould be mighty sure. And even a good start to a pension too.'

That hit home. He searched for another question. Then went: 'And how long will it take?'

'Six months: Max. You pay the ten grand now. Ten upon completion and she's all yours.'

Chris was working on an old couple the far side of the room. They musta been nearly deaf cos he was practically shouting. I opened the briefcase, looked for the contract, and twenty minutes later Rob was writing the cheque.

It went on like that. I closed ten couples. Hundred grand for the company and I got two commission. Not bad.

I'd thought a lot about Dyane during the day.

Then the phone rang.

It was her.

I nearly dropped it trying to answer. She said: 'Hello?'

'Hello.'

'What're you up to?'

'Just finished work. You?'

'Relaxing at home.'

'Oh yeah?'

'Yeah.'

'Where's Graham?'

'Business trip.'

'For the night?'

'Yeah, I'm lonely.'

'What do you want me to do about it?'

'Meet me.'

'There?'

'Yes. I want to be fucked hard.'

She hung up.

Christ.

Outside, I said good luck to everyone and faced for her house. The night greeted me with a strong wind. I walked by the Spanish Arch and on through Father Griffin Road. It was a late evening with the smell of seaweed drifting over the Prom.

I got to her house and knocked, formal, like I was delivering milk. She answered. No small talk, made my move. She was naked except for a silk robe. Tore it off and found soft, luscious breasts. Her skin was oiled and slippy and her bedroom was a dark shade of pink. Her legs came around my hips and I entered her against the wall. Up close, her eyelashes were long and her hair smelled like cinnamon.

After, we lay back panting. 'Thought you said you couldn't have an affair?'

'I've changed my mind, obviously.'

'Was it worth it?'

'Graham's not back til tomorrow. I'll tell you then.'

'That mean I'm stayin?'

'Only if you want to.' She got worried for a second. 'I'm searching for guilt, but can't find any.'

'That's cos you don't love him.'

'But I should.'

'Why?'

'Cos we've been going out so long.'

'You think that should make you love him?'

'Yeah...I mean, I thought over time...'

'That he'd grow on you?'

She stared at me. 'No, that he'd change.'

'Will you leave him?'

'And do what?'

'Live.'

'I am living.'

'You think you're livin. But you're really dreamin about what it's like to live.'

'I don't get it.'

'Me neither. I just sorta said it.'

She smiled, thought and said: 'There's a sadness in your eyes. It was the first thing I noticed about you.'

'Right now, I'm fairly fuckin happy.'

'But not always. I can tell.'

She leaned in and kissed me. Her lips were cold and tasted like lip balm. My mind was empty, like it just got flushed. The night outside was silent. She buried her head in my shoulder and threw her hand across my chest. Her breathing got heavy. We were cooling down. I pulled the duvet over us. It all felt like calm.

*Had Aslan in the head, The Gallery.*

Monday came round. I was feeling new born and truly laid. Dyane and Graham had been going out five years. They hadn't slept together in about eighteen months. She was looking for a way out. Putting it off. I don't know.

Chris rang, asked: 'D'ya want to go drinkin for the day?'

'It's only two o'clock.'

'When did that ever stop ya?'

'Where are you now?'

'*Rabbitte's.*'

Got there. We sat at the bar and slugged hard. It tasted good. I paid for two more and said to him: 'That Jennings fella was on to me the other night.'

He frowned, said: 'Again?'

'Yeah. In *The King's Head.*'

'The prick. What did he want?'

'He was actin quare, but he knows a lot about the company...'

He thought, said: 'Don't worry bout it.'

'Think'll he tell the Guards?'

'No. Sure it's technically legal once people sign the contract. Worst that can happen is we get investigated for fraud. The first hint of that and we'll close up shop and open under a new name next year. Happened before.' He took another drink, then said: 'How'd ya get on with that one the other night?'

'Dyane? Mighty. Ridin all weekend.'

'I was talkin to this one at The Oracle's place the other day. Was down for a bitta weed.'

'Oh yeah?'

'Yeah, got her number. Might give her a shout.'

'Do. What's her name?'

'Nikki Henson.'

'Cool fuckin name.'

'I know.'

Went on a crawl. Did *Tig Colí. Neachtain's. The Skeff. Garvey's. Fox's* and *O'Connell's.* Nikki arrived around nine.

Tall. Beautiful. Blue jeans, heels and bracelets. From somewhere around Westside. Magnetic smile. Wavy blonde hair. Style like a model. He held doors for her. She laughed at all his jokes. That kinda thing. She wanted to club in *Halo*. So we went to *Halo*.

Two floors in the place and plenty of pillars. Lots of fellas in checkered shirts and aftershave. They were mostly breakfast roll types with too many chins. The women brushed them off with frustrated experience. After a while, I felt unsteady, like I was on a rocky boat to the Aran Islands. Stomach queasy. Drank vodka mixed with red lemonade and ice. Good kick, like potent liquid rust. Went to the bar for more. Drank it. Things were getting blurred.

Chris was gone somewhere with Nikki.

Was on me own. Surrounded by pigs and rams. Big holes and bad style and the music was cat. Made for the door ta fuck. Outside, I was hit with a breeze. I'd forgotten my jacket. Lit a smoke and went towards *Supermacs* and straight down Shop Street. Had notions of going to Dyane's place but was having trouble keeping steady. Used the wall for support. Guts doing somersaults. Pure bushted. Puked outside *Brown Thomas*. After, I stood up and felt extra dizzy, like the boat had hit some big waves. A girl caught me by the arm, asked: 'Are you ok?'

She had a phone in her hand. I said: 'Wha?'

'Are you alright? You dropped your phone.'

She had big blue eyes and red hair and a huge pair of tits. Her fella was behind her. Arms folded. Something happened and I fell over. Hit the ground with a bang that shoulda hurt. She tried to catch me on the way down, but we both fell into the vomit. Then the boyfriend was in. 'C'mon ta fuck will ya? He's just drunk. He'll be alright.'

'But we should help him, bring him somewhere.'

'Will ya c'mon! Fuck him.' He pulled her away.

'Hang on.' She said. She ran back and handed me the phone and a fistful of change. 'Get a cuppa tea for yourself.'

And then they were gone.

I tried to stand up. Put my hand in the puke. Brushed it off my pants. Had *Aslan* in the head singing *The Gallery*.

Blank.

Then I'm having a piss outside *Powell's* music shop. Folks walked past behind me, whistling. Shouting. Giving a running fuckin commentary. I zipped up and turned to face a pair of bright yellow Gardaí. One said: 'Would ya do that in you own house?'

The worst kind. A woman.

The other was the tall, silent type. He was like a telephone pole. I attempted an apology with: '...huh?'

They let it digest, looked at each other and said something I didn't catch. Then the fella said: 'I'm giving you a choice, lad: either you give me an address or you're spending the night in a cell.'

Tried to give my address. It went like this: '...huh...?'

She moved in fairly swift but there was no need. I couldn't've defended myself against a tin of beans. On the way to the car, hands twisted behind me, someone else started talking. I thought it was another Guard, but recognised the voice. 'I'm responsible for this man. What's the problem?'

The tall one turned. 'Are you his father?'

'Yes. Sorry Guard. I'll take him out of the way now. There's no need to bring him in.'

The bitch turned. 'He was abusive towards the Gardaí and refused to co-operate when we offered to bring him home. I think there's every need to bring him in, and issue a summons.'

'I understand that, but he has a chronic alcohol problem and court is not the place for him. Please, let me take care of it. I'll have him off the streets in an hour.'

She kept her stern tone. 'If I see him again tonight, I'm bringing him straight to the station.'

They let me go and my arms came alive with pins and needles. I was feeling cold and car sick. Turned and saw Jennings waiting. Long coat and greasy hair shining. I said: 'What the fuck are you doin here?'

'You looked like you needed help.'

'Not yours, thanks.'

I tried to walk. Took one step forward and stumbled backwards. Nothing behind me. He ran to make the catch but I'd already hit the ground. And I'll tell ya one thing, drink or no drink, it was fuckin sore.

*Foosterin'*


Woke up on a floor. Covered in a blanket. It felt like early morning. My mouth was dry, like I was after drinking a pint of sand. Inside my head, there was intense pain, as if my brain had teeth and someone was drilling them all. I sat up with bleary eyes. There was a smell of cigarettes, and something wet, like an old raincoat. Still in my clothes, stomach bad, like it was wishing for botulism.

Flashbacks of *The King's Head* and *Halo* and cop uniforms.

Someone said: 'You're awake.'

It was Jennings. Sitting on an old chair, looking like he was after being dug up. 'What the fuck am I doin here?'

'Better than a cell.'

I looked around. 'If you say so.'

'You were so drunk you couldn't walk. I did you a favour.'

'You dirty bastard. You were probably tryin to interfere with me when I was asleep.'

'Don't talk shite. Someone needs to explain to you what's properly goin on.'

I took a fit of trying to stand, weathered a head rush. 'Where's the door?'

'You don't need it yet.'

He had a point. I was dizzy as fuck. I sat down again. 'Have you a cuppa tea at least?'

'Hang on.'

He went to the kitchen. Foostered around. There was a lot of rattling of press doors and rinsing of cups. He came back and left it on the table. It was a dirty mug with a big red heart on the face. There were streaks of brown cemented tea on the side. He sat back opposite me and said: 'I want to talk to you about Frank Rowland.'

'Who's Frank Rowland? I don't even who the fuck that is.'

'How can you not know? There's no property. No contacts in Bulgaria. Nothin. It's all just a scam. Ten grand for a weekend in a cheap hotel...'

'So now I know. I still don't care.'

'Why not?'

'Why would I? Why would *you*? People can do what they want with their own money.'

'How's your woman?'

'Dyane?'

'Yeah.'

'Why?'

'She might be in trouble.'

'How?'

'Frank is mental. You wouldn't know what he'd do. And he has enemies too, lookin for a way to hurt him.'

'Why would anyone do anythin to Dyane?'

Jennings shrugged. 'It's just the way these things go sometimes.'

I looked around. An old record player in the corner. Furniture all tattered like rotten cabbage. Wallpaper ripped and torn. Battered looking window with a damp spongy frame. Went: 'Have *you* nothin better for doin?'

'No. We should talk about *Fisherman's Blues*.'

'The song?'

'The place.'

'It's a place?'

'Yeah.'

'I think you're touched.'

'You won't soon.'

'When?'

'When she's gone.'

'Sound. I'll get back to you when she does.'

'I'm serious.'

'So am I.'

I left the cup on a geriatric wooden table.

Jennings said: 'How can you not care about anythin I've to say?'

'Cos it's either shite. Or it doesn't make a difference. And now I've to go.'

And I went.

*Cheap dirty gold.*

The handle on the door looked like cheap dirty gold. It closed behind me with a light clap. Dingy stairwell and a smell of mould.

Outside. Breeze. Bright. Afternoon hell. He lived by the station. Smell of exhaust and piss as I walked towards the square. Tremors in my hands and a loud drumming in my chest. Angry morning traffic clogged the streets. A couple walked past, arguing about missing a bus. The sun was out and my armpits were wet and sticky. There was no doubt about it: I was pure sick from drink.

Took a long route home. Walked through Eglington Street and on towards Bowling Green. Pale enough sky, whispered rain. Punishing wind, cold enough to be white hot. Puke always threatened. Passed Nora Barnacle's house and into Dominic Street. The walk felt good, almost like exercise.

At the flat, the place was quiet, but unsettled. Nothing seemed familiar, like a cloned reality. I pulled the curtains and turned off the light. There was a smell like dried grease. I tried to chill, but everything seemed like an act to keep off an avalanche. Lied back on the couch, mind like an icy road. Walls of panic either side. Slept a bit and woke up in a bad way. Terrible fear. Felt thinner, like I'd lost two stone in my sleep. Nightmares followed me into consciousness. Rabid dogs and killer viruses and zombies. Sleep Paralysis and *The Hag* like a scorned incubi. JOBbridge were in there too.

Looked at the ceiling for a while. My shirt was stuck to my back in a film of sweat and everything was silent.

Got up and went to the radio and put on some *Athlete - Chances*. It moved me somehow, like a teardrop fell from my heart. I lit a smoke with shaking hands. It tasted dry. Didn't want tea, but I boiled the kettle anyway. Lied back on the couch again. Put one arm over my eyes like I was blocking out the sun. Checked my phone. Missed calls and messages from Chris and

Dyane. Rang her back, no answer. Paranoia set in. Somewhere a dark cloud gathered, brewing up a catastrophe.

Finished the smoke. Rang her again. She answered. Her voice making pure shite of the hangover. 'Hey, sorry....'

'Everythin alright?'

'Yeah. No... I'm fighting with Graham.'

I'd forgotten he was still a factor. Said: 'Fuck him, get out of the house. Let's go somewhere.'

'I'm not really in the mood...'

'I know a good Indian place.'

She thought, said: 'I love Indian.'

'C'mon so.'

Had a shower. Put on some *Aslan*. Felt even better. Gelled the hair and left.

—

Met her outside the courthouse. She had a bag in one hand and put the other under the crook of my arm. She was dressed in a short skirt, denim jacket, hair in a tiny ponytail. Green eyes sparkling in the streetlight. I wanted her there and then. We went to a place on Quay Street. Her heels echoed on the cobbles while we walked.

There. It was dark red, smelled of curry and candlewax. Statues with gold chains. Our table had a candle and a green tablecloth. A punter came down, looked like Gandhi, gave us the menus. I ordered the Lamb Tikka. She went for the vegetarian. He asked about drinks and I got a bottle of cider. She went for the *Pinot Grigio*. Always with the big shtuff.

After he left, I asked: 'Do you like this place?'

She sighed 'Yeah, it's alright.' Pause. 'But I hate conversations about the quality of the food and the style of the restaurant. I want dinner to be about something other than filling silence.'

'Like what?'

'Were you ever in love?'

'No.'

'Tell me about the first girl you were ever really with. You know what I mean.'

'It was nothin special. Graham your first?'

'Yeah, right.'

'You seem sheltered.'

'Go fuck yourself. There's a difference between privileged and sheltered.'

'So rich people sleep around all the time?'

'No. They're normal, that's all. And *I'm* not rich. *He* is.' Beat. 'What're your parents like?'

'They're great. What's your worst fear?'

'Dying alone.'

'What makes you think you could die alone?'

'It's so easy for a guy to say that. Women get traded in for younger models all the time.'

Gandhi came with the drinks. Left them down. I filled her wine. Got working on my cider. She said: 'Name a fantasy.'

'*Harry Potter.*'

'A sexual one, stupid.'

'Jesus.'

'You embarrassed?'

'I'm not sure what you're askin me.'

'Ok, I'll tell you mine.' She took a drink. 'I want to be fucked when I least expect it.'

The surrounding tables got interested. I took a long pull of the cider, said: 'I think some people call that rape.'

She took another sip. Small mouth. Eye lashes. Painted nails. Impeccable manners. 'Not necessarily *rape*. I'm talking about being in the house on my own, bored, not expecting anyone, and then suddenly I'm being rode senseless.'

'Who's goin to ride you if you're in the house on your own?'

'He's going to break in.'

'Oh right.'

'Yeah. I told Graham and he called me things I won't repeat. I thought he was going to shit.'

'It's not exactly normal.'

'It's just role-play.'

Beat. I thought about it. Then said: 'So, you're on your own, like on a Wednesday night or somethin...'

'It's winter.'

'It's winter, and...'

'Ok, I'll explain. It's winter. I'm bored. Alone. And there's no prospect of meeting anyone for the rest of the night. It's like I'm in the country or something. I'm sick of reading, and watching television, and sending messages and I start thinking about sex. It's so unlikely that I want it more than ever. It's not like I want to make love, I just want to be fucked, hard and long and forceful. I don't want to see the guy's face so it's better if he wears a balaclava. The bedroom would be too formal and ruin the excitement so we could just do it wherever I am at the time. Say, the kitchen table, or the stairs, no, the stairs would hurt my back. Say the living room floor or something.

There's no foreplay, or dialogue, and I even try to resist, but he gets the better of me and then I just relent and let him have his way. I want it to last, so the guy has to have stamina. As I start to climax, I want him to squeeze my throat, not choke me, but have a good grip. Then I want him to fuck me harder until I climax at least twice more and then he's allowed to ejaculate.' Beat. 'My fantasy's complete as I feel his erection break and his cum flood inside me.'

'And he's a stranger?'

'No. You missed the words "role-play." Who knows what I could pick up from a stranger? And besides that *is* rape. He'd most likely be a boyfriend, or at least someone I enjoy fucking. When we're finished, he just gets up and walks out and I don't want to hear from him again until at least the next day.'

A middle-aged couple behind us were looking uncomfortable. I asked: 'And you don't think that's weird?'

'Everybody's weird, if that's what you want to call it. Some people are just more open about it than others, but everyone's got some kind of secret desire.'

She looked out the window, then right at me. Her eyes again.

'It's more natural than strange, maybe not conventional, but I'm not ashamed.' Smile, then: 'Why should I be?'

39

—

We ended up at the Spanish Arch. It was a cool, quiet night. A group of hippy types played guitar in the corner and the smell of hash floated over, like burnt fur. The water was shallow but still had a strong current. We sat back on the grass. Her eyes told me she was merry. She said: 'I like feeling alive again.'

I wanted a drag of that joint. Her hair tickled the side of my neck. A breeze came and she shivered and threw her bare leg over my knee. She had the scent of an orchard in summer. I finished my smoke and threw it away, rushing water, said: 'I want to spend more time with you.'

Later, in her room, the moonlight shone through the open window. A fan whirred in the corner and our clothes lay scattered on the ground. The smell of incense lingered from a used stick on the dresser and I watched the reflected light, from the cars outside, float across the ceiling. Dyane's breathing came in contented heaves. When she spoke, it came as a murmur. 'This is intense, Jack.'

'I know.'

'What are we going to do when it ends?'

'Why're you thinkin like that?'

'Because it always ends.'

'Maybe we can beat it this time.'

'How?'

'I don't know.'

'I hope you're still here in the morning.'

'I will be.'

'Good night.'

'You're beautiful.'

'Thanks. You're sweet.'

'Move in with me.'

She didn't answer.

*Some of them are awful innocent.*

*Pink Floyd - Hey You.* Shaking trees. Falling leaves. Wet streets. I was back in the hotel the following weekend. Sold twenty false apartments. There'd been an incident in the morning when some fella went mad cos he knew it was all a fix. But other than that it worked out alright. Chaplin said good work and he paid us and I went for a pint with Chris in *The Dew Drop*.

Nice *Guinness*, lots of corners and Europeans with hats and scarves. A smell of hops and ale. We took a seat by the door. Asked Chris. 'How're you gettin on with Nikki?'

'Sound. Probably stay at her place tonight. You sell many today?'

'Bout twenty. You?'

'Same. Nice dusht.'

'Tis. It can't go on forever, though.'

'I know.' He said. 'Did you see your man this mornin goin mental?'

'I did. He nearly hit me a shlap.'

'Fuck.'

I asked: 'Did you ever feel guilty about it?'

'About wha? *Workin*?'

'Takin the money.'

'Heh?'

'It's like robbin...'

'No, it's not. Sure that's all there is in the world. People sellin bullshit to other people that are stupid enough to buy it.'

'Shtill. Some of them are awful innocent.'

'No one forces them to sign anythin. There's no fake signatures. Fuck them if they're too thick to know they're gettin screwed. They deserve it as far as I'm concerned. Did I tell you John Hanover rang me?'

'Who?'

'Your man that was supposed to get your job insteada you.'

'Oh yeah. Him. What you tell him?'

'He was wonderin what the shtory was. I told him there was a mistake. No job for him after all. He said he was goin complainin to JOBbridge. I told him to belt away. He sounded like he was a bit fucked up anyway. How's Dyane?'

'Dyane? Shtop. Deadly.'

He took a drink, said: 'See. You wouldn't have met her unless for the job.'

'No. I suppose not.'

'And you wouldn't have the job only for the fuck up with Hanover.'

'Fair point.'

'So who would you prefer to be seein her? Him or you? Feel guilty all you want but think about that when you're ridin her tonight. Chaos is a cunt for some people but fuckin great for others. Depends on how you look at it.'

'Chaos?'

'Yeah. Chaos Theory. Somethin happened years ago that set the whole lot in motion. One of our customers went down one street instead of another. Found a shop. Went in to buy somethin. Met the love of his/her life and it all kicks off and they get married and want to invest in somethin for the future. And now we're here payin for the pints with their pensions. And they'll have kids that'll grow up and join the fraud squad and close down companies like ours cos they heard what happened their oul pair. But by then we'll be long gone.'

My phone rang. I looked at it, said: 'This is her now.'

Went outside to answer, she said: 'Hey, I did it.'

'What?'

'Left Graham.'

'Left him?'

'Yeah.'

'How'd he take it?'

'I wrote him a letter.'

'And?'

'He phoned and called me a cunt and told me to go fuck myself.'

'How you feelin?'

'Like I've been cured from a terminal illness.'

'Want to meet?'

'I'm outside *O'Malley's* on Prospect Hill.'

'We're in *The Dew Drop*. I'll come up and meet ya there....'

Click.

Chris waited, tapping his knee, looking around. The place was getting busy. He asked: 'She comin in?'

'No. I'll go and meet her.'

'Sound. I've to get ready to meet Nikki anyway.'

Shop Street assaulted me with good vibes. The buzz of new beginnings. I walked fast, smoking at the same time. It was like crossing a bridge from a world of winters to a much better climate. Threw my smoke in a puddle and gave a homeless fella my change.

There was a long queue outside *Cuba*\*. It began to rain. I hurried on. Lotsa drunken young ones outside *Vivo*, letting themselves go.

She looked outta place, but not uncomfortable. Blue jeans, red jumper, runners. I asked: 'What's with the style change?'

'Process of reinvention. I want a pint of cider.'

'Sure we'll have one in *Richardson's*.'

Got there. High ceiling. A line of chairs. Old geysers working on philosophical pints and time killing whisky. I asked her: 'What're ya havin? Cider so?'

'Yeah.'

'Sound. Me too.'

Bought them. 'What'll we toast to? Us?'

'And the end of him.'

Her hair down, her eyes bright. She was a portrait. We left the pints on the counter. I asked: 'You think he's heartbroken?'

'I doubt it.'

'Where ya gonna live?'

'With whoever will put me up.'

'That'd be my place so.'

She leaned in closer, hands in tiny pockets. 'How was work?'

'Totally illegal.'

'So are you going to be a con man forever?'

'You're talkin forever?'

'Just curious.'

Tunes kicked in, *The Ramones - Pet Cemetery*. Had electric vibes throughout my body, like I'd discovered the meaning of life. She said: 'You don't think it's too soon for me to move in?'

'Where else are you goin to go?'

'I don't know. A hostel or something.'

'And do what? Fuck that. We're goin home after this.'

Shortly after. We made the trek back to the flat. The house sang of silent excitement, a nervous energy in the air, like lots of invisible pets had been waiting for us to return. Her bags made a loud *whump* against the wall. We loitered in the moment. Her eyes wide with dilated cider. I kissed her. We went to the bedroom and turned off the light. And I was thinking:

John Hanover can truly go fuck himself.

—

Woke up to a new world. One where white noise no longer existed. Dyane lay naked against me. Her pale face was serene in the dim light. She opened her eyes, like a newly born kitten, closed them again and fell back to sleep. Cars grumbled by outside. The hiss of a bus. I went to the bathroom. Stepped over her underwear on the floor. Brushed my teeth. Thought about crazy things, like a floating dead goldfish I'd once gotten as a birthday present.

Came back and my mobile was ringing and Dyane was gone. The bed was empty and cold. I looked around. Out in the kitchen. On the couch. Opened the door and glanced down the hall. Nothing. No sign of her at all. My legs were shaking. The phone kept going. I answered. It was Chaplin. He opened with: 'Well, bollox?'

'Hello.'

'Who the fuck is John Hanover, eh?'

'I don't know.'

'Ya know fuckin well.'

'What are ya on about?'

'That's it now.'

'What?'

'It's all fucked.'

'What the fuck're you sayin?'

'Hotel. Apartments. Bulgaria. End of story.'

'Sure what's the problem?'

'JOBbridge were here. They've it all put together. Closed us down entirely. Can't operate. Out of the job because of you, ya little fuckin...'

'Ah, hang on a second....'

'Seen your doll lately?'

'Who?'

'Dyane, the little cunt...'

'How do *you* know about Dyane...?'

'Cos if *we* go, *she* goes. Like I said, it's all fucked. We're all off to *Fisherman's Blues*.'

'Are you on drugs or somethin?'

'Why the fuck didn't you just stay in Ballinrobe where ya belonged....?'

He didn't hang up, but the phone went eerily dead, like a candle that was blown out. I looked at the ground. There was a stain on the floor like the shape of Ireland. The toilet gurgled. I looked at the empty bed. At the ocean of roaring absence and warmth that was there a few minutes ago. Where the fuck was she gone?

I rang Chris. He answered, in a bad way. 'I woke up and Nikki was gone.'

'Yeah! Dyane's fuckin gone too.'

'What the hell is goin on?!'

'Chaplin rang.'

'Does he know about Hanover?'

'Yeah. Said JOBbridge were down and closed the whole shop.'

'Fuck!'

'What are we gonna do?'

'How the fuck do I know?'

'What's goin to happen to *us*?'

'Haven't a clue.'

'I'm worried.'

'So you fuckin should be. What about the women?'

'I went to the bathroom, came back, Dyane had disappeared.'

'Entirely?'

I looked around: Clothes, jewellery, everything gone. 'Yeah.'

'We'll have to meet somewhere. How was Chaplin?'

'Thick as fuck. On about *Fisherman's Blues*.'

'What the fuck's he on about that for?'

'I don't know. I don't even know what it is.'

'It's a fuckin song, ya dickhead.'

'I know but...'

'Fuck him. We'll go to *Neachtain's*.'

'Sound.'

'Sound.'

'See ya there. Sound.'

'Sound.'

'Fuck. Right. Sound.'

'G'luck. Sound.'

Click.

The shock was wearing off. The fear was setting in. Was afraid parts of me were going to start disappearing, like when time travel gets tricky and the universe collapses. There was no sign she'd been in the house, that she'd ever even existed. I checked my phone and her number was erased. I knew only two things: I had to find her.

And I was dying for a pint.

So I got dressed and went to *Neachtain's*.

*I'd a feelin this might happen.*


Exterior. Outside *Neachtain's*. Lots of beards and wicker chairs and thin cigarettes. Burshted in the door. The hiss of flowing ale. A smell of soup and coal. I got the round, asked Chris: 'What do ya think?'

'I tried to ring Chaplin, there. He's gone now too.'

'Jesus. Where the fuck do people go?'

'I don't know. I never seen the likes of it.'

'Me neither. Bollox anyway.' I took a hit, said: 'Decent *Guinness*.'

'Not bad, yeah. Hanover must have caused a right fuss. God knows where we'll end up now.'

'The prick.'

Chris shouted two more. 'We're left around for somethin all the same.'

'How d'ya mean?'

'Like... all the rest of them are gone, but we're still here, talkin, so if we're in some kind of Bermuda triangle shtuff then they don't want us, whoever the fuck *they* are....'

'I know, sure Dyane was savage. No wonder they took her.... how can she just disappear, though?!'

'You wouldn't know in the fuck. Sure same fuckin thing with Nikki.'

Thump of heavy pints on wood. A warm fire, heats up your jeans til they get too hot and burn the back of your legs. Fella at the bar turned around. His name was Spike. He said: 'How's things?'

I gave a sullen howya. He continued. 'Did I hear ye say you're missin someone?'

I gave him the outlines. He said: 'I know just the man.'

'How d'ya mean?'

'To sort ye out.'

Chris asked: 'Sure how can we get sorted out? They're gone.'

He took out his phone. Talked. Hung up and said: 'Don't go anywhere.'

So we didn't go anywhere. Drank a fair bit. An hour later, Jennings walked in. Smell of wet socks and stale piss. Long fingernails and jaundiced eyes. Cheap jeans, worse shirt. He wheezed: 'I'd a feelin this might happen. Howya, Spike?'

'Kurt.'

'Will ya have a pint?'

'Go on, so.'

He called a round. I asked: 'Where'd *you* get money?'

He answered thick with: 'In my pocket.'

'What's the plan so, smarthole?'

'Any sign of the women since?'

Chris said: 'No.'

He got pensive with: 'I took a walk passed the hotel there, too. Gone.'

I took a long belt of porther. Trad session starting in the corner. Accordion clearing it's throat. Jennings took off his jacket, rolled a thin smoke. He was playing man of the moment. Trying to heighten the drama. Milk the attention. He held up the cigarette and licked it and said: 'I'm goin outside to smoke this.'

I went: 'Come back with a plan. We're stuck for a future.'

'Relax, relax.'

He walked out. Chris said: 'Suddenly he's a fuckin Buddhist.'

'He's the best.' Said Spike.

'Best at what?' I asked. 'Talkin shite?'

'He'll get ye the wheels ye need?'

'What the fuck do we want wheels for?'

'To get the women back. There's only one kinda car that can go there?'

'Where?'

'The next level.'

'Have another pint, Spike. What the fuck are you on about?'

'Ye'll see.'

Jennings came back and said: 'I had to think about whether I wanted to do this or not. I had to think long and hard. There's a lot at stake...'

Chris said: 'Shtop talkin shite and tell us...'

'When I was young...'

'Oh for fuck's sake! Where are we goin?'

Spike cut in: 'It's like goin into a Black Hole. No one ever sees you again. No one knows what's on the other side.'

I swamped the pint, asked: 'And that's where the women are?'

'Yeah.'

'What's it called?'

Jennings went for grave with: *'Fisherman's Blues.'*

Chris looked at me and rolled his eyes and muttered: '... Shtop...'

Spike said: 'It's a song by *The Waterboys*, too.'

Things were getting mental. I called a round of *Jameson*. Asked Jennings to explain. A fella came in from outside. Rain coming off his opened umbrella, dripping on the ground. The trad session kicked off. Accordion going strong. People tapping their feet. Delighted Germans drinking glasses of *Guinness*. PhD types in the corner, froth on their bushy lips.

The *Jameson* went down warm, kicked the tonsils on the way. Jennings went for more drama. An old man telling young men an unfortunate tale. It was taking too long. He turned round and I drank his whisky. He copped on after that, started trying to make sense.

He said me taking Hanover's job had interrupted something serious in the chaotic spectrum and we needed to make it right. It was all about going through a special door somewhere. You had to find it in a particular way and only a certain car could achieve the force and centre of gravity required to make the leap through. It was going to be dangerous, terrifying, daring, but we had no choice. There was silence. Spike said: 'All ye need is the balls and the car.'

I asked: 'What kinda car is it?'

Jennings said: 'Opel Astra. 1994. Has to be silver to reflect the intense heat of the Particle Warp. It was discovered by a couple of Lithuanians a few years ago but they didn't know its true value and sold it to me. I'd spent years lookin for it...'

'And they just gave it to ya?'

'No.' He said. *'DoneDeal.'*

'Ever used it?'

'Not yet. I'm terrified.'

Chris said: 'I'd be terrified too. The fuckin thing is over twenty years old!"

For the first time, I saw Jennings angry. 'It's *thee* Silver Opel Astra, 1994! It's not just some normal fuckin...shitbox!'

The pub went quiet. Kinda got the feeling it was a yarn he told Americans to get free drink. Up there with Leprechauns, Banshees and Pishogues. There was only one thing to do. Chris said: 'We're goin to need to see it.'

'Tomorrow.' Said Jennings.

'Why not now?'

He gave it a second. Then said: 'Cos this is the last session we might ever have.'

I asked: 'What's in it for you? Why would *you* go there?'

'That's personal.'

Spike wanted to know if he could come too. We thought: Why not? Bought more whisky. Big drink. I was worried about Dyane. Wondered where she was. If she was waiting for me somewhere. Chris said Nikki was: 'The besht fuckin girl he'd ever met.'

Spike called it a 'Mission from God!'

Jennings tried to sing but the bouncer said he was shite, and if he didn't shut up he'd get barred. So he stopped singing and got kinda sulky and sat on his own for a while. Eventually he came back for the next round of *Jameson*.

We asked the fella behind the counter for some *Waterboys* but he said it was bad luck and he wouldn't play it so we got a bag of cans and went back to the flat. Through the cold night and the rain and the gnawing wind. Jennings said they didn't have rain where we were going. I asked him how he knew that and he said he read it in a book. I asked him what book but he wouldn't tell me.

The busker was on Shop Street. He was kind of Spanish or something. We brought him home. He was delighted to get inside and drink with us for a while. He played a few acoustic numbers and then we asked him for *Fisherman's Blues*. He went kinda pale. We gave him the outlines of the story and he said: 'You kies are fuckeeen crazeee...no?'

But he played the song anyway. Said it was the only time he'd ever play it cos it was a serious occasion. He put in the perfect notes. Perfect tune. Lyrics all on cue. We listened, like it was a sweet siren calling from a terrible place in the far beyond and we knew that we would never be the same again after this. Like it was our last night before a terrible run into a hopeless war.

I went to hug him after, with tears in my eyes, but my shoelaces were open and I fell over and busht my head off the side of the couch and didn't wake up again for the next thirteen hours.

At that stage he was long gone.

Cuntish.

## Shlabs of Bavaria

Jennings shook me awake with: 'Jack, are ya right?!'

Opened my drink poisoned eyes and the first thing I thought about was Dyane.

Her scent.

Her body.

Her hair.

Felt like I was built from radioactive emptiness. Sharp hollow pain.

Warm sun through the window. An empty bottle of *Jameson* on the floor. My stomach flipped, like a dying fish on dry land. Jennings kept shaking me, saying: 'C'mon...we have to get the car...'

I stood up. Felt dodgy. Gave the couch a stern look and asked: 'Where's the fuckin busker gone?'

'Gone.'

'Gone where?'

'How the fuck do I know? Chris is on the way back with breakfast rolls.'

'That might do the job.'

'Then we have to get the Astra.'

'Where is it?'

'*Tonery's.*'

'What's it doin there?'

'I hid it.'

'Why?'

'Cos it's the most valuable artifact known to man. That's why.'

'Shtop. What time we leavin?'

'After the breakfast, we'll go to *Aldi*, get some booze, and then we're set.'

'*Aldi.*'

'What's wrong with that?'

'Nothin.'

'D'ya want a cup of tea?'

'No, I want to find Dyane. Fuck it anyway. How are we gettin to this place?'

'It's complicated.'

'How complicated?'

'Cuntish enough.'

'Far?'

'Not really.'

'Where's Spike?'

'*Neachtain's.*'

'Is he still comin?'

'I think so.'

Chris arrived with the breakfast rolls. Silver torpedoes of cholesterol. We lashed them open. Rashers, sausage, pudding, the works. Chewed hard. Relished. After, felt a bit better. Drank tea and smoked. Chris said: 'So the car's in *Tonery's*?'

'Behind it.'

'Sound, we'll go there first, collect it, stop at *Aldi* and get goin. Any idea how we're gettin there?'

I looked at Jennings. He looked at the ground and said again: 'It's complicated.'

—

The day was bright. Lots of people shopping and talking on their mobiles. Walked passed *Abrakebabra* and the entrance for Corbett Court. The sweet sound of a harp near Shop Street. There was a girl playing it on the square, long hair, mittens on her tiny hands. Chris said her name was Annie Chambers. She had a crowd, but didn't seem to mind. Gave her a tenner and kept going. Christ, I was loaded these days. We all lit smokes. Grey nicotine and a tinge of self-hurt. Took a right on Prospect Hill. Chris asked Jennings: 'Do you reckon they have reception there?'

'How the fuck should I know?'

'Well you seem to know everythin else about the fuckin place.'

'Piss off.'

Chris took out his phone. Dialed. Listened. 'It's ringin!'

We all stopped to see. Huddled in and heard: 'Hello?'

Big excitement. 'Hello, Nikki?'

'No, this is her friend, Sarah. She left her phone here. Have you seen her today actually cos usually she....'

'Aragh, shite.' Said Chris.

And he hung up.

We walked on with heavy hearts. A light drizzle began. Galway rain, unique in the world, speaks volumes, melts on the streets like memories, plays on the cobble like piano keys.

*Tonery's* was orange and closed. There was a car park out the back. We got there. Found a gate. Jennings had a key. We entered. Rusty hinges. Loud squeal. Smell of oxidation. Puddles. Potholes. Trees. A path through the middle.

We pushed on. A large warehouse. Padlock. Another key. Opened it.

The Astra was inside. A mechanical diamond. Impressive physique. Untarnished silver. New tires. Polished lights. The place was empty besides. Smell of spilled oil and bird shit. I asked Jennings: 'Who owns this place?'

'I used to. When I wore a younger man's clothes.'

Chris said: 'Open her up to fuck.'

We sat in. Comfort. Clean dash. Tape deck with a jack for hooking up your Mp3 player. There was a discussion about who should drive. None of us trusted Jennings. Chris was still on his provisional license.

It came down to me: Fuck it. I'll do it.

We pulled out. She was a beast. Wanted to roar ahead. Sensitive to the touch of the foot. Power steering. Motorised personality. We roared into *Aldi*. Envious looks. Shtuck her in the disabled spot and attacked the off licence inside. Shlabs of *Bavaria, Fosters, Firkin Brau, Stolichnaya vodka*. A few bottles of *Country Spring* Lemonade. Filled the boot and most of the back seat. Got food too.

*Doritos.*

A loaf of bread.

Dodgy butter.

Twenty cans of beans.

We were set.

Rang Spike. He said: 'I think I'll stick here. The craic is good.'

'Sure?'

'Fuck it, yeah, I've to sign on the dole tomorrow, and if I miss it again they'll cut me straight off.'

'Sound.'

Hung up. Found a €50 fine on the windscreen for not having a disabled permit. Gave it to Jennings. He said: 'Shite!' and put it in his pocket.

I said: 'So tell us the next step. What's the plan?'

He finally told us how we were going to go through his special fuckin door. After, I looked at Chris. He was staring at a puddle on the ground. I turned back and asked: 'Which roundabout?'

'Headford Road.'

'And we have to *what?*'

'Drive around it.'

'Ok, and tell me the rest again...?'

'We have to drive around it the wrong way. In the opposite direction like...'

Chris asked: 'Jennings, are you fuckin serious?'

'Very fuckin serious.'

'Where'd you get this idea from?'

'I heard it.'

'Where?'

'St. Mary's.'

'The fuckin mental home?'

'I was in for drink a few years back and a fella in there told me.'

'Better get the *Bavaria*, Chris.'

'Hang on,' said Jennings. 'It's true. He said he was there. He'd done it. Swore by it.'

'And what happens if a big fuckin artic lorry arrives?'

'It won't if we go fast enough.'

I lit a Benson. Let the smoke go through and exhaled. A bruised cloud in the Menlo distance. The Astra was getting bored. A clunk came from somewhere inside it. I asked: 'How fast?'

'Once you hit fifth in the car it's supposed to reach faster than the speed of light. We go round it sixty times. It should take less than half a millisecond at that speed. Then you veer to the centre of the roundabout and the door opens and you go through.'

Chris sparked a can, slugged, said: 'Astra. Speed of light. Wrong way round the fuckin Headford Road roundabout, sure what could be simpler?'

Jennings checked his pockets, said: 'Fuck it, I'm outta fags, have ya got one?'

I gave him one. His fingers were brown. I took out a can, sank it fast. Tasted like my first Holy Communion. When the oul fella went to the jacks and I drank his pint. He came back and I thought he was going to kick my hole. Instead, he said: "Fair fucks to ya, you're well able for it...."

Irish dads.

Can't bate them.

Chris said: 'Right, are we doin this or what? These fuckin women better be there.'

We all sat in. Kinda awkward, like this was a stupid idea but no one wanted to say it. I started her up and she roared. Put it in first and crept towards the Headford Road. The most important thing was to find a quiet moment, when the cars were few. Pity it was one of the busiest spots in the country. And that no one really understood roundabouts anyway, just kinda drove on and hoped for the best.

A truck trundled past, its trailer bouncing in delight. The lights went red at the Limerick exit and I sank the shoe.

Thing is about driving in Ireland, soon's ya do something erratic, everyone starts beeping, pointing; thinks they're a motorological fuckin genius.

No one could believe what they were seeing.

A fat woman in an SUV.

A suit and glasses in an Audi.

A scumbag in a Honda Civic.

Their faces said: He's American.

Stupid.

A fuckin eejit.

Doing his driving test.

All of the above. And mental.

The beeping got louder. Everyone flashing their lights and trying to say: 'You're doin it wrong!'

Like we didn't fuckin know.

We got to fourth on the first spin around. A mad man with an umbrella trying to wave us down. A siren wailed, but we were going too fast to see it. Narrowly missed a motorbike by the sign for Dublin. He managed a demented swerve and disappeared. Everything started to blur. The cars less solid, stretched before the eyes. Head getting dizzy. Jennings shouted: 'Do it!'

I gave it a second, afraid, then shoved her into fifth and faced for the middle. There was an almighty explosion of light and sound and intense energy. And then everything went black and we weren't even real anymore. Dematerialized into some kinda bright particles. No sound, no taste, no touch. Just a floatless drift into somewhere we couldn't see. And for a second I knew everything. I knew the meaning of life, the world, of people. I knew what death was. I knew the nature of existence. I knew what it was to transcend and revisit the point of conception.

And then we landed, in a dramatic crash, and the Astra bounced on to something that felt like welcome tarmacadam. Chris was screaming in the passenger seat and all around us there was sand, just a vast landscape of sand. And a blue sky and a lonely small cyclone of brown grains. There was a hiss too cos some of the cans had burst in the back.

The car was still running and there was a long endless road stretching ahead. A grey path through the desert. Jennings said: 'I thought we were dead.'

'I think we are.' Said Chris.

I looked around, asked: 'What now?'

'Fucked if I know,' said Jennings.

So I put her in first and drove.

*Dave.*

*It'd be nice to hear a bit about Nikki too.*

The crescendo arrived and I shot my load, in her mouth, like a glorious death. After, I fell back on a bed of dark truth, letting it ride, watching the ceiling, letting the rain of pleasure fall, like hot flakes of stardust.

She stayed there a while, making sure. Then, beside me, she said: 'You're one of the nicer fellas.'

That voice. Resigned to a life of purchased love. I tried to think of an answer. Something wise and paternal. My phone rang. I let it go. It went again. Checked it. Kirby the cop. I answered. There were no formalities. Only: Had I heard about Nikki Henson?

A tirade of emotional hieroglyphics. Then I asked: 'What about her?'

'Fuckin kidnapped.'

'Was she fuck?'

'She fuckin was.'

'When?'

'She left her house and disappeared.'

'Fuck me.'

Pale light across the brothel floor. A car slushing through a puddle outside. Then: the rebounding silence of a bedroom in winter. Belt buckle and cold shadows. On the phone, there was a blast of something in the background. Photocopiers. Office world. He said: 'I've to go, Dave.'

And he went.

The whore asked me: 'Is everything ok?'

'Not really.'

She seemed sad, continued with: 'Did you have a good time?'

That voice. I got up. The bedclothes weren't heavy. There was rain on the window. I was feeling light blue and holographic. A mantelpiece on the back wall. Cigarettes in the grate beneath. A smell like must and old tobacco. I picked up my jeans. My hands were shaking. Nikki Henson. What the fuck.

Took out a couple of purple notes. Left them on the locker beside the bed. There was a lampshade and a lighter and some coins. A cheap bracelet and a broken fake fingernail. Marilyn. That was her name. She asked, unsure: 'Do you want change?'

'No. No change.'

My shirt was on the ground. Checked the time. It was fuckin late. Car keys on the floor beside my shoes. Picked them up and got working on the laces. Soon was set to go. She hadn't moved much, cept to take the money and put it under the pillow. After, she blinked. Her eyes loyal to anything else I might want. She watched me buckle the belt. Someone's daughter. Someone's sister. Maybe someone's mother. I was ready to go. I looked at her. Something forming. Could've been pity. She felt it and turned her back and I left. Such are the swings.

The door was heavy. The stairs windy. The lobby was empty, like a sad man's dreams. The Galway night was cold, with plenty of rain. It hit hard, like every day guilt. My car was the far side of the road. Black Honda Civic. Did the job grand. Sat in. Started her up. Got some heat going and drove on through the ugly night. The wipers doing their thing. Thoughts of Marilyn fading, like the echo of a good song.

—

Indicated on to Mill Street and took a right down Dominic. Decided to start with some local contacts. Caught Larry at *The Galleon* in Salthill. He was working hard on a steak. A bored brunette beside him. She was seventeen at best. Her legs crossed. Larry always liked them young. I looked around. It was getting busy. A smell of dried grease and burnt coffee

He went: 'How's things?'

I shrugged, pulled over a seat and said: 'I want to talk about the thing with Nikki Henson.'

'You and the whole fuckin world.'

'You hear anythin?'

'I heard she was kidnapped.'

'That all?'

'That's all I know.'

Close up the girl looked even younger. A generous fifteen. Pale face and chewing gum. I'd seen her around before. A sad creature. I focused on Larry, said: 'I got the call an hour ago.'

'I thought you might be on it alright.'

'What can you do?'

'Fuck all. Can't you see me and Sarah-Jane are tryin to enjoy a romantic meal together?'

That was her name. Sarah-Jane. She sighed, then grabbed her bag off the table and took out a phone. I got a whiff of cigarettes and disco. Larry scraped up some fat and chips. Ate it and swallowed. Then he sat back and took out smokes and sparked. Twenty Carrolls. He offered, but I said no. Got some funny looks and whispers from a couple of cappuccinos in the corner. He gave me a deadpan stare and said: 'This is serious.'

'As opposed to what? A circus?'

He blew a cloud in my direction. 'You read the papers lately?'

'I never read the papers.'

'There's a fella just out of Mountjoy.'

'And?'

'He went down years ago. Had a serious crew.'

'What was he in for?'

'Drugs.'

'So he's out. What has that to do with Nikki?'

'Think about it.'

I did. Nothing happened. I said: 'Larry, will you get to the fuckin point?'

'Somethin to do with Ice and Heroin and a fucker named Tycho. That's all I heard.'

'Tycho?'

'Yeah. "Tycho the Psycho" they call him. There's talk that he wants to decimate Frank Rowland.'

'Why?'

'Cos he's mental.'

'Frank?'

'Both of them. Tycho's into some kinda Black Mass... Voodoo shit, too, just like Rowland, so at least they have that in common.'

The bouncer landed, not Irish, pointed at the smoke. Larry gave him a look of death and I sensed there was going to be violence. Time to leave. Put a donation in Larry's top pocket and hit the Galway air.

Ice and Heroin. Rowland never went for that. High risk and too little reward. Would only destroy the city with junkies. Probably why Tycho the fuckhead was making a move against him.

Walked on.

Outside the Bank of Ireland. Rain still coming, like tears for my lost night at the brothel. Orange streetlight bouncing off the puddles. Casino dreams bouncing in the distance. Drunk students across the road. Puking. Shouting. Acting like they were on an American film.

The killer was standing against my Honda. Long brown coat, like an extra for *The Untouchables*. Hands in his pockets. He was watching the students. Particularly the drunk women. I was up behind him before he knew it. Put my gun to the back of his head and pulled the trigger. Silencer on, no big sonic boom. His skull cracked with the bullet, like the sound of a coconut breaking.

I picked him up and bundled him in to the boot. There was blood and brains on the ground, but the rain washed it away. Took his wallet. Made a mental note to go through it later. Knew it would tell a story. I had a feeling these cunts were hard, but amateurs.

Back behind the wheel, I lit a smoke. Major. Tasted strong, like vindication. Turned the ignition and got some *Interpol* going: *Narc*. It sounded good, like a compliment to the scene. Taking the turn towards town, I felt him roll around in the back. Took a long drag and exhaled into the wet road of St. Mary's night. Wanted to get rid of the body. Knew just the man to call. I dialed and he answered with: '...Surprise sur fuckin prise....'

*Nothing Escobar.*

The Ferryman said he'd need an hour. Figured I'd call on Robin while I waited. Got to Knocknacarra. The lights through my windshield; reminded me of Vegas. Robin was an average dealer in smoke. She had some regulars and it paid the bills. Nothing Escobar, but her clients were the type to talk and she was a good listener.

She answered in black hipsters and a tight top. Let me in with a smile and a size eight swerve. She took to the kitchen and I went to the living room. Yellow paint and tall cabinets. Expensive looking crystal inside. Checked out the pictures on the wall. Portraits of horses, and boats in windy seas. Photos of her folks and their pet dog.

Took a seat on a red leather couch and lit a smoke. She arrived in, sipping a glass of wine and asked: 'Did you bring fags?'

I threw her a Major and she sparked it and didn't flinch. Some woman.

'So, what the fuck're ya doin out here?'

Potent nicotine in the air.

'The job on Nikki Henson.'

'Heard about it. Happy Rowland no doubt...'

'It bein his daughter and all...'

'Why is she Henson if the father's Rowland?'

'Somethin to do with the mother.'

Wooden floor. When she walked, her high heels echoed. She took a seat and crossed her legs. Her eyes were wide like moons and her large round earnings gave her a gypsy edge.

She blew smoke and said: 'I never really liked Nikki that much....'

'That's immaterial.'

'She fucked around a lot.'

'She got a lot of attention.'

'Maybe she fucked the wrong fella. Or maybe she's gone.'

'Dead?'

'No. Spain or somewhere.'

'I doubt it.'

'With a father like *hers*. And a life like *this*. Why not?'

'Same as me and you. It's built in. We're fuckin lifers.'

'So why would anyone kidnap her?'

'Someone's actin the cunt. Have you heard of any new gangs movin up here, anythin like that?'

She took a sip. Those legs. Black curls. 'I'm busier, if that's what you mean.'

'New customers?'

'Yeah. One from Mayo. I don't trust him.'

'Why not?'

'I don't know. Talks a lot about Tycho somebody. Wants to know where I get my gear.' She thought, said: 'His hands are all fucked up, too.'

'Why's he want to know where you get your gear?'

'Notions about bein a dealer I think....I told him to talk to The Oracle.'

I looked around, asked: 'Where's the teacher?'

'We broke up.'

'That's a pity.'

'Is it really though?'

'I don't fuckin know.'

She dragged hard, asked: 'You workin right now?'

'Yeah. Have to meet a fella in town.'

'D'ya want to call out after?'

I thought about Marilyn. The overlap. Said: 'It could be late?'

She blew some smoke. Tipped ash into the fire and said: 'I'll wait up. I'm doin fuck all else....'

Cruised back into town and called The Ferryman. He said he was ready. I put on sounds. *The Black Keys* came through the speakers with *Psychotic Girl*. It went well over the speed ramps. The night had an air of expectancy, like the world was waiting for something to happen. Went passed *Seapoint* Casino and up to the docks. Met him at the Dun Aengus side. He was pulling in a boat. The sound of lapping water. The smell of seaweed. Indifferent ships. A green light flashing in the distance. A dead body in my boot.

I walked over. Through the biting wind and the drizzle. My ears cold. Hands in my jeans pockets.

The Ferryman was old. Beard. Long black coat and yellow teeth. Wispy grey hair. He opened with: 'It's busy out there tonight.'

'Boats?'

'Dead bodies.'

'Who's bringin them in?'

'I don't ask. How many do you have?'

'One. Fairly fresh from this evenin.'

'Money up front?'

'Put it on the tab.'

'About that...'

He was wearing white torn shoes. His fingernails were black. His eyes cracked with red thunder and mortal understanding.

I said: 'You know I'm good for it.'

'Only as long as you're alive.'

'What's your point?'

'Things aren't too certain, there's...talk.'

'About wha?'

'All I know is I've never been so busy, and that's a sure sign of war.'

'I hear ya, but you don't need to worry. If you want, sum it up and I'll have it for ya next time.'

He nodded, said: 'Thanks, Dave.'

'Hear anythin about Nikki?'

'Did you love her?'

'Didn't everyone. Why're you talkin about her in the past tense? Was she here?'

'No. You bringin me somethin?'

I took the body from the boot and dragged it over by the legs. He was heavier than he looked. Noticed a tattoo on his arm, couldn't make it out in the light but it looked like a swastika. The Ferryman asked: 'You talk to Rowland?'

'No, but he'll want news soon.'

I pointed at the dead man: 'Any idea who he might be?'

'I tend to stay outta this feudal shit...'

'Know anythin about tattoos?'

'Not much. Why?'

I took the arm. The sleeve was wet. Pulled it up and said: 'Look at this...'

He blinked, said: 'I've seen this before.'

'Where?'

'Jail.'

'Who are they?'

'It's a satanic gang. Run by a prick called Tycho.'

I thought about that. Three hits. Larry, Robin and now. He went on: 'He was an animal. Did some inhuman shit to people.'

'Even you?'

'Especially me.'

'What do you think he's doin in Galway?'

'He was always ambitious.'

'What's he into?'

'Everythin.'

'What about Ice, Heroin, that kinda shit?'

'Like I said: Everythin. Probably reckons he's goin to take on Frank Rowland and recruit every daft bastard in Hell to help him....'

'That's the least he'll need for a move like that...'

'Here, pull that cunt over. I'm busy...'

He took a machete from the darkness. I left the body by the water's edge, head hanging over the dock. The Ferryman started on the arms. High, hard attacks. Blood spattered. Bones crunched. He stood up, out of breath; legs spread, and sincerely asked me: 'D'you want to stay and watch?'

Back at the car, it was almost time to call Rowland. I opened the dead man's wallet. There was a couple hundred cash. I kept that. Nothing else except an expensive card for a place called *The Red Dragon*.

So I started up the car and went there.

*Head like an onion.*

*The Red Dragon* sounded Chinese. It wasn't. Black door. Blood walls. Just behind *Monroe's*, by the bridge. Parked the car and lit a Major. The wipers stopped half way, frozen there, looking scared. The engine ticked, cooling down. I was feeling cold. Thought more about Nikki. She was mixed up but I liked her. She was one of our own. I tipped ash by the gearstick. The sky was dark, like a rotten gum. My mouth was dry and some new angry rain battered the roof and buttered the window like silver sludge. The history between me and Nikki was short but intense. I'd had her. Everyone had *had* her. I liked to think it meant something. So did all the others. Things changed when she walked into a room. The furniture hushed. The music faltered.

I took another long pull of the smoke. It was warm between my fingers. A couple walked past, sharing a jacket over their heads.

Nikki chose me. I don't know why. I liked to keep things quiet. Maybe that was it. First night we were together, I knew she was trouble. My drink had danced the second she sat down. Her perfume got into my blood and I knew I was in the grip of something dangerous. Such are the swings. She ordered two *Jameson*. We drank them and fucked later. She lived alone. A one bedroom place. Mattress on the floor. It was a complicated thing and it was summer. The days were humid. The blankets always damp with sweat and fluids. Her father wouldn't like it. We made nothing public. She liked to smoke at the window. The cars cruising by on the dry road beneath. She'd sit in profile. Legs to her chin. Having me watch her. This is how she lived. Through the fantasy and memory of others. I thought we wouldn't last and I was right. One day I left her place and knew I'd never return. She knew it too. Such are the swings. At the bar, when she started leaving with other fellas again, I tried not to mind. Then one day I heard a flake she was with had beat her up. Someone had said he was great on the guitar. Like

Mark Knopfler but better. So a couple of nights later I dragged him down an alley and shot him in both hands and told him why. He bled into the rain and cried like a newborn child. It felt fuckin great. I'm sure there's a name for this kind of behaviour. Somewhere in a book somewhere. Who cares.

I could still see the outline of *The Red Dragon* through the tsunamic window. A freak wind blew and gave the car a turbulent shake. I got out and the breeze attacked me like a wet plague of locusts. It went under my collar. Fed on my knuckles and burnt the skin of my jaw. The tip of the cigarette flared with the sudden blast of oxygen. I took one last delight and threw it away into the dead atomic night. The river flowed angry under the bridge, like a liquid stampede.

At *The Red Dragon*. There were two bouncers at the door. Overweight and bald. Hands clasped like they were at mass. I approached with: 'Lads?'

Close up, they were squat and ugly. All garlic gums and arrogance. One was fairly hoarse. He said: 'Do you have an invitation?'

'No. Not really.'

He chewed on something. Looked over my head and said: 'No entry without an invite.'

'Why not? I'm just lookin for a beer. What's the problem?'

'There are other pubs.'

'I want to try somethin new.'

The second one turned and said: 'Well try somewhere else. Now...fuck off.'

I raised my hands and said: 'Ok so, ye touchy cunts, relax....'

Took a walk around the corner and tried the back door instead. Negative. Then. The exit flew open and a waitress walked through, blonde and cute and holding two bags of rubbish. She gave me the eye and threw the bags in the skip. She was walking back when I said: 'How much does a man have to pay to walk through that door?'

She stopped and thought. 'That depends. Many men pay with their lives.'

'Gimme a figure.'

'A straight hundred.'

'How's about fifty and a kiss?'

'No thanks.'

She was going away again til I said: 'Ok, let's do it.'

'Money up front.'

There was a canopy overhead. We stood under it to stay dry. I took out my wad and shaved the notes. Her eyes were hungry, like she wished she'd asked for more. I handed it over with: 'Lead the way, babe.'

'Use your fuckin head. They can't see me walkin you in. Give it a minute. I'll leave the door off the latch. After that, we never met. Does that sound like somethin you can understand?'

She smelled like cigarettes and *Jameson*. I said: 'Whatever.'

After some waiting. I went inside. The lights were dim. Everything the colour of red wine. Black stools and awkward modern chairs. Candles on the tables. Along the left was a long shining bar. A smell of *Jaggermister* and varnish. *Bill Withers* on the speakers with *Lovely day*. Figure that.

A young lad stood watching bored horseracing on a big television. He noticed me and got to attention. I ordered a double brandy. He hesitated, like he was about to ask me for I.D. Then he got it. I floored the drink and got another. Told him to take one for himself. He did, then went to the phone. The night was getting expensive. Thank fuck for the dead fella's €200. The brandy roared inside me. I asked the kid: 'Who's the boss of this place?'

He was uncertain, then said: 'I don't know. I just work here. Hang around til some of the lads come. They might be able to help you...'

'Who's the lads?'

'They're behind you.'

And they were.

*Like a narcoleptic on ketamine.*

Looked back. There was two punters in leather jackets on the approach. The first fella walked ahead with all the confidence of bad films. A tower of bryllcream and aftershave. Going for the Alec Baldwin look. The other one was just a fat cunt. Baldwin said: 'You must be Dave.'

I turned, went: 'Who are you? Mystic Meg?'

'No, just good at what I do.'

'What's that, then?'

'Who the fuck let you in?'

I took out the Coconut's wallet, left it on the counter, showed him the card, let the logic take hold. Then said: 'Where's Nikki Henson?'

Logic wasn't Baldwin's strong point cos he said: 'Fuck you.'

'My boss doesn't accept them kind of answers.'

He went for cheese with: 'Maybe he won't be around for much longer.'

'Unfortunately you're wrong. God love ya.'

The kid's face went back and over like this was a game of table tennis. The bulldog behind Baldwin had a head like an onion. I gave him a wink, then shot him through my coat pocket. I'd screwed off the silencer, so the bang was loud, and even *Bill Withers* seemed to stutter on the chorus for a second. The Onion dropped, like a narcoleptic on ketamine, holding his knee. I pointed the pocket at Baldwin and went: 'I think we should bring this conversation to the next level....'

The kid had ducked behind the counter. Hands to his ears. Baldwin got all Hollywood with: 'You're goin to get killed for this.'

'Enough fuckin prophecies. Tell me where Nikki is.'

'Even if I knew for sure I wouldn't tell you.'

'Why not?'

'Cos you're goin to kill me anyway.'

'Maybe you're a bit psychic after all.'

He went for his gun and I shot him. The Onion looked up at me, like a dying donkey. I lit a smoke and saw the blonde was watching from a balcony above. She looked scared. The kid behind the counter was having something like an epileptic fit on the floor. Shivering and crying and blubbering. I said: 'Hey, Shackleton...'

He looked up.

'...You be sure to tell Tycho what you saw....d'yunderstand...?'

He nodded that he understood. I think. My brandy was still on the counter. I took in some Major, then drank it before I exhaled. My system approved, like I'd thrown coal on to a fire of hate inside. *Bill Withers* was just coming to the end of the song. Dragging out the *Lovely Day* bit. I left down the glass with a bang and shot the Onion in the heart and hit the road. The same bouncers were at the door on the way out. I said: 'Thanks, lads.' And they looked at me like I was an apparition.

Got back to the Honda and tore away thinking: 'I'm flat out killin fuckers, and still no sign of Nikki.'

*Motorcycle emptiness on the radio.*

In the city, it was time to visit the boss. Drove on through the flaking rain. Hard to know if the weather was normal or the first signs of a wonderful storm. Could go either way.

Rowland had a modest place beside the canal. Richest criminal in the country but never flashed it.

Arrived a few minutes later. There was a punter standing outside with a shotgun. He watched me approach and made a request on his earpiece. After, he listened, nodded, and opened the door. I walked through the hallway. The walls were white, with pictures of prize winning horses.

His only indulgence.

An equestrian centre in Kinvara.

He was in a room at the end. It smelled like incense. Oak table with a picture of Nikki. Big blues eyes and blonde hair. A natural beauty. Sea behind her. Some holiday somewhere with her mother. A glimpse of a life I'd tasted once, but where I didn't belong.

The room had low lighting. Television on the back wall, leather chair facing it. I stood and waited to be received. He was flicking through news, share prices and race meetings. After a minute, he opened with: 'Go on.'

Gave him the highlights. Finished with: 'I'm fairly sure these fuckers have her.'

'But you don't know where she is?'

'No. Not yet. But I think they're into some kinda Satanist shit.'

'Why?'

'Larry mentioned it...thinks it might be connected to your relationship with God.'

He turned around, said: 'But I haven't spoken to God in ten years?'

I shrugged, went for the Ferryman's theory and said: 'It's possible Tycho wants to break into new territory but can't do

it without some supernatural help....so he's practicin some....
dark arts....'

'Could be the other way around, the dark arts usin him....'

I hadn't thought of that, went: 'How d'ya want to handle it
from here?'

'We have to find her first.'

'Any requests for a ransom or anythin?'

'No. What did the Guards say?'

'Rang to tell me. But that's it so far.'

'Maybe they know somethin by now?'

The other walls were a pale light blue. He left down the
controls. Thick hair and grey stubble. Broad shoulders, wearing
a suit. Steely blue eyes, like Nikki's. I owed the man a lot.

He said: 'You feelin calm?'

I shifted my feet, said: 'Calculated.'

He looked at the picture on the table. 'That's my fuckin
daughter, Dave.'

I felt a twinge. Did some emotional alchemy. Converted it to
rage. He continued. 'They say she was fuckin some fella that
worked in one of my hotels, what do you think of that?'

'Which hotel?'

'The Bulgarian thing.'

'I'll check it out.'

He handed me a card, said: 'This is the place. I want you to
send your cop friend down there. Kirby.'

'Why?'

'Cos this Tycho prick could be there with his crew waiting
for you to materialise. They won't shoot a Guard. At least, I
hope they're not that fuckin stupid. Tell him to bring a squad
car. Do that and get back to me.'

Out through the hall. Back to the Honda. My ears got wet.
Rain rolled off my jacket, shone in the moonlight. I was feeling
tired, maybe old. In the car, the mirror showed grey stubble.
How bout that. Sorta yellow smile. These things just happen,
sure as the night comes. I turned the key with a cold hand. My
wrist ached. Leather squealed. Fuck the seatbelt. Put it in first.
Faced it for Mill Street. Got there. Sparked another Major. My

chest liked it, my heart not so much. *Motorcycle Emptiness* on the radio.

—

I pulled up and let the car cool down while I waited for Kirby. Somewhere in the night, a pair of high heels clicked past, like a walk to an innocent dream. I thought more about Nikki.

One day in her apartment.

Few months back.

It was bright outside. Sunlight draped along the floor. That smell of sex and perfume. She smoked at the window. Tried to tell me about a past lover. I didn't want to know but she told me anyway. He worked in a bank. Treated her like a doll. I smoked. Watched her ceiling, trying to make an excuse to leave. He'd brought her to Italy. A place called Florence. There were exotic buildings and lots of art. He was selfish in bed. She was never satisfied and she used to roam the streets when he slept. The Italian cobbles. The ghostly fog. The way the men used to look at her from late night doors. Red lit windows and the low throb of music. Sometimes it was Jazz. Others Dance. The lyricism of the language. The lament of lost possibility. She felt the breath of the continent come around her. There was no Atlantic bitterness. Just the exotic smells and the cultural borders. She was hoping to get gang banged but it didn't happen.

When they came home. She ran him. He didn't understand. Her fellas never did. She looked at me on the ground. Her face drenched in unreal sun. She wanted to go back to Florence. Did I want to go? Did I fuck. She stared for a few seconds and thought about saying something. Then she didn't. Just looked back out the window. I had another smoke and studied the ceiling. There were shapes by the light like piss and countries. Her legs were brown and she mighta been crying but I didn't care cos I knew she was playing a part. Some film she saw. Some war flick or wild European romance where she's the victim and she's always left unfulfilled. And them silent tears are bringing back a memory of a deep wound or emptiness. And I'd played my part good too. Somehow proved to her that she lived in a hopeless world. Hopeless for a girl like her with dreams like that and ambitions for Jazz and Hollywood and scandal and, who knows, she might even get to fuck a president someday.

But no.

She was here with me and the Galway breeze blowing light on her tan legs and her lips getting cracked from pulling on those old smokes all day long. And she wonders about what might have been or what might be yet if only she could....and she just didn't know what that thing was. Is. Will ever be. She could only dream and use fellas like me to try and find it. And then the car door opened and Kirby got in and I stopped thinking about Nikki for a while.

—

He had thick black hair and a suit. A wet folder with something inside. Pulled the door shut like a man jumping into a bunker from a warzone. He said: 'Some fuckin weather.'

'Tis.'

'Fuckin Arch is flooded. Half the station down there. Divertin traffic.'

'What's that in your hand?'

'How's Rowland?'

'How the fuck do ya think?'

'That Nikki was mental.'

'Try *is* mental for now.'

'Sorry.'

I smoked harder. It danced on my tongue. Bounced off my windpipe the whole way down. Terrible affliction. He took out a picture of Tycho. Bald snake with dark eyes and a big nose. 'Tycho the psycho. Locked up for fifteen years. All the usual shite. Killed cunts. Drugs. Rape. An all rounder.'

'What's his story now?'

'It's like he's after gettin his PhD. Fifteen years in there is like the best education a criminal can get.'

'Why Galway?'

'That's where Nikki gets involved.'

'Keep goin.'

'He's not long out. Has a brother. Hangs around *Freddie's* pub. His name's Jesse. Plays the guitar. Dreams a lot. Harmless enough. We arrested him once or twice. Nothin serious. Some small time dealin in weed.'

'Weed?'

'Yeah. Then Tycho gets out and the waves start comin. He was bad years ago. Now he's insane. I mean the term literally.'

'Get to the bit about Nikki.'

'It's the brother: Jesse. She fucked him for a while. He wanted more. She didn't. He didn't like it. Then he gets drunk one night and kicks the shite out of her.'

'I heard about that.'

'Thing bein, this fella's a musician. Gifted or somethin. Then he gets shot in both hands. Never goin to play again.'

I had a craving for vodka and diluted orange. Christ, it caught me hard. *Freddie's* might be doing some late booze.

I said: 'So Tycho thinks his brother's hands are all Nikki's fault.'

'Fuckin right. They say that's the only way to get to Tycho, through the brother. He fucks up anybody that hurts him. He's a total sociopath besides, but, touch the brother and he gets a bit human.'

'Anythin about Satan?'

He gave me a look, said: 'Yeah. How'd you know?'

'What is it?'

'He calls his crew *The Red Dragons*, but they're fairly amateur in that line. Black Masses, sacrificed a few kids, burnt a couple of churches, an inverted crucifixion last year....suspected of a mass rape in a convent....'

'That's *amateur?*'

He shrugged, said: 'Who gives a fuck about his hobbies? He wants to flood Galway with his cheap Ice and Heroin. And he wants to hurt Rowland for cripplin the brother, and the two just happen to be linked...obviously kidnappin Nikki fits into that equation too.....'

I gave him the business card for the hotel and hit the wipers and said: 'I need you to check out this place.'

'What is it?'

'Last fella Nikki was fuckin. He worked there.'

He looked at the card. 'This is one of Rowland's hotels.'

'Tis. Let me know how get on.'

'Why can't *you* go?'

'I'm less expendable.'

A squad car pulled into the station. A homeless fella walked passed. His back wet. His head studying the cracks on the ground. I was grinding my teeth. That kid with the hands. He screamed something at the time. "I'll get you, you're dead." The usual. Had I known, I'd've finished him off. You live and you learn.

I turned the ignition, said: 'I've to go.'

'How's Robin?'

Kirby always liked Robin. 'She's not too bad.'

He put the card in his pocket. His phone rang. He looked at it. 'Probably more fuckin floods.'

I twisted the key again. It started. A calm roar. Kirby was still staring out the window at the grey waterfalls rolling down. I knew the look, asked: 'How long's it been?'

'Six months.'

'And the family?'

'What fuckin family anymore?'

'If it wasn't for Rowland you'd have concrete shoes.'

'And no more debts.'

'You can blame the roulette for that. And the booze.'

'Who are you? "Doctor Bob"?'

'Go fuck yourself.'

'I'll call you later.'

He opened the door and walked into the night. I pulled away. Thinking bout that vodka and orange and the wisdom to know the difference. Might try another brandy instead.

## *Do you never get lonely?*

Back at Robin's. The brandy inside me. Blood roaring for more. She was better than I remembered: Agile, energetic, passionate. Later, I was spent. We lay naked together, smoking. She said: 'Ever get sick of the life, Dave?'

'Never stopped to think about it.'

'*I* do.'

'Your sins are small.'

'I still don't like it. Do you never get lonely?'

'My conscience is all the company I need.'

'It's no way to live.'

'I do alright.'

'Things could be better.'

'I doubt it.'

'The teacher wanted to make things work. Make a go of it.'

'Why didn't ya?'

'I'm holdin out for you.'

There was a noise outside. I reached for my gun and was dressed in seconds. Robin sat up in the bed with: 'Who the fuck's that?'

I walked to the balcony. A shape. A shadow. It was Kirby. I'd almost shot him before I realised. Then I said: 'How the fuck'd you know I was here?'

'Your boss did. Rowland. He's outside.'

'Are you back on the sauce?'

'No. I'm serious.'

'Rowland's outside?'

'Yeah.'

'Outside my house?' Asked Robin.

Kirby was pale. Not looking good. I said: 'You alright?'

'I went to the hotel.'

'And?'

'And we should talk about *Fisherman's Blues*.'

Robin was still confused. 'What's that got to do with anythin?'

'Let's talk to Rowland first.'

He walked back down the stairs, then turned and said: 'Oh, and Nikki's dead by the way.'

# The road to Limbo.

The sun dipped. Dark arrived. Dead wind. Chris was asleep. Head back, half a bag of Doritos in his lap. The road stretched ahead. Coulda been to eternity. Jennings hadn't said anything for a while. I looked back and he was picking his nose and throwing the snot out the window.

Hours passed like that.

It was just me and the road and thoughts about home and Dyane. And whether I'd ever see her again. Then Jennings spoke with. 'Where are we goin to sleep?'

It had never occurred to any of us. We had booze, and beans, but no sleeping bags. Fuck it. Hit the brakes for a second, kinda hard, enough to jerk Chris awake. He came to life and grabbed the bag of Doritos like someone was trying to steal them. There was a big crunch of tin foil. Then he said: 'What the fuck sorta driving are you doin?'

'We're tryin to decide where to sleep.'

He looked around. 'Here in the car?'

Jennings said: 'Not a bad idea.'

I said: 'It'll be too hot for all of us.'

Parked up. Got out to stretch. Feeling beat and tired and lost. There were crumbs of stone but no life. No insects crawling. No tress stirring in the distance. Nothing. The sky was a dome of stars. An orange halo rested along the horizon. I walked onto the hot desert and sat down and felt an odd comfort. The sand was like a soft bed and it was warm enough without a blanket. The Astra was alongside me on the road, faithful as a good dog, a proud protector. I told the lads I'd be sleeping outside, they could have the car.

After a few minutes of silent boredom, I got a *Bavaria* and sparked it. Took a long slug beside the boot and burped. Looked at my shoes, grains of sand in the laces. Drank more. It was far from smooth. Thought again about Dyane. Was she dead or alive? Chris was gone back asleep, but he was snoring.

Jennings was twisting and turning. Eventually he landed out with a can for himself.

We were well into the *Stolichnaya* and lemonade when he said: 'That *Country Spring* is pure piss.'

'Like drinkin bog water...sure we might as well drink the vodka straight.'

Silence. Then I said: 'You're like a man that has a story.'

'Every man has a story.'

'But yours has ya turned inside out.'

'You're right there.'

'And what was that about you bein in St. Mary's for the drink?'

'I wish that's all it was.'

'Go on, sure. Talkin cured a lot of things before St. Mary's ever came along.'

'Twas a woman of course.' I let him go on. He said: 'I was a teacher.'

'*You* were a teacher?'

He let the surprise slide, said: 'Yeah.'

'Sorry, keep goin.'

'I'm used to it.'

I took a belt of the turpentine, winced and asked: 'Could you not handle the pressure?'

'Not that.'

'The students gettin to ya?'

'Her name was Kohlia.'

'What the fuck sorta name is that?'

'I never found out, as much heartbreak as it caused me.'

'Was she a girlfriend, like?'

'Pupil.'

I looked at the car, at my thumb over the rim of the bottle, then said: 'Oh, right.'

'She was older than the rest.'

'Fuckin hope so.'

'16.'

'And you were?'

'31.'

I thought about that. Took another hit of the *Stoli*. It was like a kick from a gypsy's horse. I shuddered and said: 'Tell me the rest, sure.'

*She married the woodwork teacher a year later.*

He got ready to speak. Swallowed hard and assembled the story. Talked like he was describing a film in his mind. His eyes turned inward, watching the scenes go by. 'I was a professional. Admired. Passionate. She was young, highly intelligent. I'd never seen a mind like hers.'

'So ye hooked up?'

'She wanted grinds.'

'What did you teach?'

'Maths. I've a PhD in Quantum Mechanics but there's not much use for it in Ireland.'

'Better it's gettin.'

'Hey! If ya don't want to fuckin hear it....!'

'Go on, go on!'

He swallowed, too far gone to stop. 'It was the usual fuckin story. November. Warm fire. My house. Her legs. Us alone. No one giving two fucks about the maths. She didn't need grinds any more than I did.'

'And...'

'The parents were gone away for the night. We were in her place. Bottle of Gin and the whole night ahead. It was all set. But when it came to it, I turned away.'

'Why?'

'I had morals at the time. And they got to me.'

'How'd she take it?'

'Never said a thing. We never actually spoke about it.'

'Huh?'

'The parents landed home. It was awful late. They knew well what was goin on and they ran me. Even though nothin had happened, I shouldn't've been there. Drinkin with her. Compromised like that. I was engaged the same year to be married. My fiancé was a teacher too. In the same school. There wasn't much money around at the time and teachin was a good job. We were all set and then I met Kohlia. And then Kohlia left. Was gone. I don't know.'

'Where'd she go?'

'They said she was moved to some other place up the country.'

'And you never saw her again?'

'That's not the point. She was inside me by then. It was like swallowin a hive of bees and every one of them was stingin me to escape...'

'Cuntish.'

'I saw her on the street. In the distance. In every passin car. At night, with my wife to be, I tried not to think about her, but...'

'Fuck.'

'Yeah. So I started drinkin kinda heavy. Didn't work. I went to hookers. Didn't work. I read hundreds of books on the psychology of obsession. And for a while she'd go, leave me alone, the torment would stop, but then, like a fuckin tsunami, it'd take over me again and I'd be lost to the black fuckin... nowhere.' He drank. Burped. 'My work suffered.'

'Fired?'

'Not at first. They let a lot of things go. But I lost patience with everyone. Students, teachers, everyone. Almost got violent. Then I came in drunk. Tried robbin the Principal's office.'

'For money?'

'To find her file, like, and figure out where she'd gone. He came in and caught me and that was that.'

'What you tell the fiancé?'

'Turned out I'd caught syphilis off one of the hookers so that was that fucked too. There was a good few talkin at that stage anyway.'

'Jesus...'

'She married the woodwork teacher a year later.'

'Who? The hooker?'

'No, ya thick cunt, my fuckin fiancé.' He contemplated his hands for a few seconds. 'Eamon Cusack. Useless creature.'

I took a drink. Then said: 'Ya fuckin eejit.'

'You don't understand torment.'

'Obviously not. Maybe you should have just banged her when you had the chance.'

'I felt it was morally wrong.'

'Even though ye connected and all that?'

'Yeah, look where my morals got me.'

'I don't know how you resisted.'

'If she hadn't left…maybe…'

'I suppose she was young all the same.'

'She was and she wasn't. It was like a one horse race and I didn't put anythin on in case I'd lose.'

'Sure you'd see your own arse with hindsight. Could you not find her at all?'

'No. Same as *ye're* women in the end. Everyone just assumed she was gone to another school, but, when I looked into it, it was like she never existed, and that's what really fucked me up.'

Took another hit. 'Was it soon after that you went to St. Mary's?'

'Twas. And your man in there told me she was out here. Waiting for me. Get the Astra, he said. Find the roundabout and go.' He looked right at me. 'So far so good.'

'Why'd you come a Private Detective then?'

'That was all shite. I bought the badge from some fella in town. "The Oracle" they call him. I thought it might help me find her, but it didn't. I wasn't that good at it, really.'

'I was thinkin. But you were investigatin the hotel?'

'I was down the dole office and I heard John Hanover complainin to your one behind the desk. Then I got curious and asked around about *Fortune Travel*. Ye were fuckin chancers in there.'

'Made a few pound all the same. Why didn't ya use the Astra until now?'

'Ye two were supposed to be with me. Your man in the mental told me there'll be two lads that lose two women and they're the ones that I'm supposed to bring. "Don't leave til then," he said.

'This fella knew a lot.'

'He'd want to know a lot, considerin who he claimed to be.'

'Who'd he claim to be?'

'I'll tell you that some other day.'

I shrugged, said: 'What's the first thing you'll say when you see Kohlia?'

'I don't know. I'll tell ya straight: I'm scared. Been scared since the day I bought the car.'

'But you're here now anyway.'

He took a drink, looked into his plastic cup, then out over the flat nowhere. 'Yeah...I'm here now anyway....now pass the fuckin bottle....'

*Ring Einstein and ask him.*

Morning comes like the Tet offensive. Jennings flat on his face, dead except for snoring. I stood up and stretched. Head sore, like it was full of poison ice cream. Dry mouth and peptic screams and the fear that I might puke a furry animal at any second. I thought about Dyane. Her moist lips. Long afternoons. Warmth and vulva.

The empty vodka bottle was on the dead ground from last night. Scattered cans. No wind, hard to relate to nature when there isn't any. Everything kind of amplified, yet coming from a distance.

Crossed the road to have a slash. The tarmac felt surreal, as if it was made from glass over a massive drop below. The piss gathered in a busy puddle, but didn't soak in.

Zipped up, feeling raped by vertigo's sister. Fuck it. Woke Chris and then we stirred Jennings. It took a while, but we eventually got going. The Astra rolled smooth, a silver confident shimmer. Chris opened a can of beans, threw the lid out the window. A small fading tingle of terrified tin. I lit a Benson. Inhaled. Bloodstream nicotine, a satisfied thirst. Hangover calming down and I was starting to feel safe. The sun got high and a blister formed on my thumb from the heat. And the road stretched on. It was obvious we were all kinda thinking the same thing. So it was time to say: '...So we're here....drove for a whole day and saw nothin. Are we just goin to do the same fuckin thing again...or what?'

'Just keep goin.' Said Jennings. 'What choice do we have?'

'Yeah, but, we don't even know where we are.'

Chris said: 'My oul fella used to talk about the Twin Paradox. You ever hear of it?'

'I don't think so, no.'

'It's about Time and Space bein relative.' Said Jennings.

'Yeah.' Said Chris. 'It was an Einstein thing. A twin leaves on a ship. Travels at the speed of light into a distant galaxy. He's gone for maybe a year. But when he gets back, forty years have passed on Earth and his twin brother is 39 years older. Understand?'

'Right.'

'So If we've traveled *here* at the speed of light, how much time has passed at home?'

'Forty years?'

'Who the fuck knows? Could be ten thousand for all we know. The future.' Beat. 'Flyin cars and cancer cured. Do you know the static that comes from your telly when there's no station.'

'White noise?'

'Yeah. Well. A certain amount of that is radiation picked up from the echo of the Big Bang.'

'So?'

'That's true.' Said Jennings.

'So turn on the radio.'

I did. There was no static. Nothing. Just blank. He said: 'So we're not somewhere in the physical Universe. Where the laws of physics apply.'

'Where are we then?'

'Who the fuck am I, Stephen Hawkins?'

'By the sound of things, yeah. So is there some way to work out where we're goin then, or where we are even?'

'No, it was just somethin I was thinkin about....'

I thought about that. Changed gear and asked: 'And what did your oul fella do? Was he some kind of scientist of somethin?'

'Not really, no.'

'No?'

'No. He used to breed donkeys in Pontoon.'

'Well that settles that, then.'

'Go fuck yourself.'

'I'd say there's been bigger bangs out of my hole on a Sunday mornin somehow....'

'Hey,' Said Jennings. 'What's that?'

'Where?'

'See it comin?'

The tall arc of a tunnel up ahead. Covered the whole width of the road. It was jagged, like an angry stone mouth. I slowed down. There was no way around it. Chris said: 'What'll we do?'

'Nothin else to do.' I said. 'It's the only road here.'

'Is it safe?' Asked Jennings.

'We'll see in a minute.'

We went through and everything went black. Pure black. No more sun or sand and no grip on the road. I did my best with the steering but the car just skidded around. Aquaplaned all over the place. We dodged walls and big stones as best we could but still hit a few and there was thumps and growls from inside the engine.

'Christ.' Said Chris. 'Where the fuck are we now?'

'Sure I don't know! Ring Einstein and ask him!'

'Aragh, fuck off.'

There was an ugly screech as we nearly tore the sump going over a big rock. 'Drive easy!' Shouted Jennings.

I could hardly hear him or see him, never mind *the road*. Eventually we got on to something like a plateau and things opened up. I hit the brakes and we skidded to an uncertain halt. Sat in the silence and looked around. It was like a car park cemented with burnt concrete.

'Jesus,' said Chris. 'Thank fuck for that.'

We got out and stood around all nervous. There was nothing except a noise somewhere in the corner. It sounded like someone in pain. We walked over and found a door that led into a room lit with candles and there were skeletons on the walls. Everything was cold and dark and my vision swam. A thumping in the distance somewhere. *Red Army Blues* by *The Waterboys* in my head.

The place was mostly like a bad film except it was real. Skulls on the floor. And bloodied rags. A smell like iron and dirty water. Something chinked, made noise, rustled and moved. We looked over and saw a man emaciated. His hands tied above him with chains. Gaunt face. Bulging big eyes. Starved arms. Tongue out. A few teeth left. He was shocked when he saw us and said: 'More of ye.'

'Heh?'

'This is where ye all come through eventually.'

'Where are we?'

'Help me first.'

'Do what?'

'Cut these chains.'

I went over. They were bolted to the dirty wall and I'd nothing to break them, went: 'I can't.'

'You're fuckin useless to me, so.' He said.

Fair point, I went: 'So tell me, where are we?'

'Hell.' He said. 'Where else?'

'Who chained you up?' Asked Chris.

'I don't know.'

'How can you not know?'

'I woke up like this.'

Jennings asked: 'How'd you mean *more of us*?'

'This is where they all go through. Lost lookin like ye. Through there.' He nodded towards a door in the corner, then said: 'Are ye part of Tycho's crowd?'

'Who's Tycho?'

'Some prick they're all on about. I thought *ye'd* know.'

'When did you see anyone last?'

'There's no time here. I don't know.'

'What were they doin?'

He coughed and heaved and spat. The chains rattled. He slumped against the wall. 'They're all dead. Like ye. Like everyone. We're all dead here. I wouldn't get too excited. I see the likes of it often enough. Although these fellas looked like fuckin eejits.'

I looked down and saw our shadows reflected in the candlelight and it reassured me somehow. He went on. 'Do you have anythin to drink?'

'No, sorry.'

'Fuck.

'What's out there, beyond that door?' Asked Jennings.

I looked over. It was a creaky old thing with a bolt and darkness the far side.

'I don't know.' He said. 'I'm just here. Forever.'

I walked towards it. He got scared: 'Don't leave yet.'

'We have to.'

'Talk a while.'

'We'll come back for you when things make more sense.'

'No. You won't.' He said. 'You haven't a notion.' He rattled the chains again. Depressed. 'What kind of God would leave me like this?'

I got curious. Went. 'Did you do somethin wrong or what?'

He let the moment settle. Then said: 'Killed the wife.'

'How?' Asked Jennings.

He paused again for effect. 'Lump hammer.'

'What she do wrong?'

He looked at the ground. 'She was gettin sick an awful lot. Down at the Medical Centre every second day.'

'You *killed* her for that?' Asked Chris.

'No. Turned out she was ridin one of the doctors.'

'Oh right.'

'The unethical cunt.'

'Did you have to use a lump hammer?'

'It was impulse.'

'And they locked you up here for that?'

'No. Afterwards, I shot myself in the heart and this is where I woke up. I know I didn't die straight away so I think I'm in a coma or somethin, waitin for things to go one way or the other.'

'Oh.' Said Chris.

'Probably the same fuckin doctor treatin me too.'

'Where'd the wife end up I wonder?'

'Heaven. No doubt about it.'

'Why?'

'Cos she was a great woman.'

'Do you want us to tell them anythin if we make it back?'

'Like what?'

'I don't know. Switch off the machine or somethin....?'

'No. Jez, no. Just tell them: I'm not one bit sorry.'

'Right. What's your name?'

'Frank. Yours?'

'Jack.'

'Nice to meet you, Jack. Are you afraid, Jack?'

'Fuckin terrified, Frank. Are you?'

'Every second.'

We broke on through. It was a corridor. Darkness, unique to this place, like a blanket or something thick and stagnant, somehow malignant, like you're in a dead body.

Chris turned to Jennings, said: 'That fella reminded me of you a bit.'

'Fuck off.'

I said: 'I wonder who's Tycho?'

'He sounds like a dog.' Said Chris.

'He was a famous astronomer,' said Jennings. 'But I doubt it's him that Frank was talkin about.'

Found another room. There was a fella sitting at a table, fuckin around with a big ball of Cocaine. He was trying to snort it but the lines kept disappearing in front of his nose. He looked like a mong so we kept going. And after that there was a man called Larry surrounded by children. And they kept singing lullabies. And then they'd say, in sweet voices. 'More money, Larry.'

And he was shouting 'What more can I give ye?!'

He had a suitcase of notes.

Ten thousand.

Hundred thousand.

Whatever they wanted. And they'd keep singing and then say: 'More money, Larry.'

And Larry had black hair. And his eyes were a piercing blue and he was maybe forty-five, and his clothes were worn. His shoes were colourful, like bowling shoes.

He told us he'd been a builder. Told the story fast and desperate. Like he was pleading with a parole officer. He had three hundred and thirty three houses built just outside Roscommon. As a businessman, he was shrewd. Worked hard, but into corruption. Got planning for land that shouldn't have been developed. Some politician looking for a vote swung it for him. The building started. It was close to a school. The local water supply got polluted with something lethal and ten children died.

There was a controversy but a few more bribes covered it up. The day he was cleared in court, he was on the way to the pub to celebrate. Coming through the park. He was in a suit. On the phone. Feeling hungry. The sun was out. The same ten kids, the dead ones, surrounded him.

They didn't scream, just sang. Soft lullabies. Soft laments. Tormented him. He couldn't escape. Came around a corner and there they were. In the pub, waiting for him. Everywhere. In the end, he started running. Soon enough he saw the bridge and jumped and he ended up here.

And here they were waiting for him.

I asked him if he'd seen two women and gave him the descriptions. He said no and then asked: 'Have ye tried downstairs?'

Downstairs. There was a smell of burnt hair and glue. We walked passed a room full of spectacles and jewellery. In the next there was a woman in labour but her legs were tied together with wire so she couldn't deliver the child. The door was locked so we couldn't get in to help her. Her screams went through my head and heart and burnt a scalded bitter memory into my brain. We walked on and blood leaked from the roof and there was human body parts on the floor. Arms. An ankle. Teeth. Machines, all grey and dull and ugly, were left around. They looked like something from an abattoir. A body hung by the leg from a chain and his throat was cut and he was bleeding out. The blood was falling into a bucket and there was a dog with two heads drinking it. I stepped on something soft and looked down and saw that it was intestines covered in maggots. A stray eye ball beside it looked up at me.

We decided to go.

—

Outside again. Tried to find our way back to the car. The dominant colours were a mixture of red and black. The ground went from cement like rubble to a sort of marshy bog. The sound of agonized screams in the distance. Grey smoke all over the place. It began to rain thick ash. I had a craving for Gin&Tonic. We were totally lost. Fuck.

Went back inside and found another room. It was cold, with torn furniture and old dirty wallpaper.

We took seats around a table. Found a candle and lit it. Chris put his hands over the flame, said: 'Fuckin cold in here.'

Jennings was in some kind of shock or awe. Eventually he said: 'This is where Kohlia used to live.'

He walked through to the next room. We followed him. Faded pictures of Kohlia and her parents. On holidays at waterfalls, and with mountains in the background. More of her and the mother. Sipping cocktails and wearing sunglasses. Bikinis and all that. Kohlia's eyes, sometimes they were bright and she was happy, others there was something wrong, something missing, the way her mouth turned down at the end of a smile. Her mother was beautiful too, like an older version of Kohlia, but her oul fella was like an uncomfortable extra. Fat with a moustache and out of place with these two rides.

Looked around. Cracked wooden floor. Fireplace. Dirty bulbs hanging from an old chain. The window was black and broken, like someone had thrown a big stone through it. It was as if we'd traveled into somewhere a thousand years ahead. I asked Jennings: 'What do you reckon?'

A noise came from upstairs. Sounded like a bed being moved. Then voices arguing.

Chris said: 'What the fuck?'

'Shss...' Said Jennings.

I looked at the floorboards. All cracks. Lime coloured dust. Holes in the nowhere beneath. Kind of place you'd expect to see scared eyes, like green marbles, staring at you.

Upstairs, the voices stopped. As sudden as they'd started. A door slammed. Stale wind came screaming around the house, into the living room. Jennings said: 'That was her parents arguin about me. And this is where I saw Kohlia for the last time.'

'Well...you better go and see if she's up there.'

He looked at me kinda sad and I knew he was scared so I said. 'I'll be down in a minute. Ye wait here. And don't fuckin go anywhere without me.'

On the way up. Things seemed to be in better condition. Got increasingly brighter, newer, more life with each new step. The jacks was fairly alright so I had a piss. Thought about stuff. Like how when I first met Dyane. And where was she now? And where was all this going at all?

I flushed, pulled up my fly and heard a sweet golden: 'Hello.'

Turned to a set of big bright blue eyes.

'Kohlia,' I said. 'How's things?'

*Better weather. New congregation. All that.*

Something more had changed in the scene. The bathroom had shaken off all the cobwebs of Hell. Kohlia was only after getting out of the shower. Wearing a towel. Christ, she was even more gorgeous in real life. She looked me up and down, strangely unsurprised. Wet hair dripping. She said: 'You've made the jump?'

'How do you mean?'

'From there, to here.'

'If you say so, but, where the fuck am I?'

'My house. Mind if I get dressed?'

'Not at all. Where'll I go?'

'Come to my room. Don't worry. Nobody can see you but me.'

Her room was fresh. A reflection of her mind. Fresh and immaculate and terribly feminine. 'Sit on the bed.' She said.

It was bouncy. I thought about that. She went about the clothes thing. Didn't seem to care I was there. I looked away anyway, studied a tormented crack on the wall. Turned back when I heard the jeans close and went: 'So.'

'I've been watching you. On your travels. I know it sounds odd, but I have. Where's Kurt?'

'Jennings? Downstairs...I think.'

'Did he tell you about me?'

'Everythin.'

'Does he still love me?'

'Never stopped.'

She smiled at that, looked at herself in the mirror, rubbed a finger below her eye. Jeans like they were sprayed on. 'Which one are you?'

'How do you mean?'

'Nikki?'

'No.'

'Then you're searching for Dyane.'

'How did you know?'

'I was in St. Mary's.'

'*You?*'

'Last year. I met God.'

'Oh right. How'd that go?'

'He told me everything.'

'Like what?'

She turned, blinked like beautiful music. 'I'll tell you downstairs.'

I asked: 'So where am I now?'

'You still don't get it?'

'No.'

'You've crossed over. To the real world again. I've been waiting for you.'

'So what, I have to bring you back with me or somethin?'

'Now you're learning.'

'How'll we do that?'

'We have to fuck.'

'What?!'

'Only messing...'

'Jesus, woman.'

She laughed. It was infectious. 'Come to the porch.'

'Where's your folks?'

'Doesn't matter. No one can see you but me, remember?'

On the way, she made tea. Offered me some but I said no. The kitchen was new. The counter shiny. Well kept.

She filled a glass of water, handed it to me, and led us to the back door. We took seats outside. She was on my right, smelling like calm serenity and a return to the womb. And then there was the sounds of life. The birds, the passing traffic, the trees rustling. Even the light cool breeze was a reminder of what living was like. She picked up my frequency, asked: 'How bad is it down there?'

'Bad enough, now.'

'Is Kurt ok?'

'Middlin.'

'I don't know why we didn't just...'

'That's what we're all kinda thinkin.'

'Maybe it'll all make sense...'

'Hopefully. So tell me what I'm doin here....'

She took a sip of the tea. Small lips. Blew the steam off the mug and left it down. A lazy black and white cat walked through the trees in the garden. There was a smell like a florists.

Then she told me her story.

She'd gone into maths herself. Never fully got over Jennings. Felt rejected. Became obsessed with Chaos theory and Quantum Mechanics and Calculus and Trigonometry. The infinity of numbers. The logic of the world. After that came meditation and the connection with mathematics and the mind, and thought processes. And then obsession with neurology. The physiological explanations of the conscious state. Then peace in religion. Some spirituality. The afterlife. One day she was studying something about a world unaffected by human influence. Determinism and the absence of free will. Then everything came down around her ears and she ended up in the mental.

She was sitting awful close to me. This was her thing. Didn't know how intoxicating she was. Drive a man mad just sitting there. Staring at me. Waiting for a comment.

I went: 'And you met God?'

The psychologists got worried when they heard about the visions. I asked her what they were. She blinked and said: 'An Opel Astra going through Hell.'

'I see.'

Soft voice. 'And Kurt was there, in Hell, looking for me.'

'Sounds a bit daft alright.'

She continued. They'd put her on medication. Prozac, and all its cousins. The visions kept coming. Fires. Desert. Angels covered in blood. She could feel Jennings sometimes. Close. Watching her. Others she was sure he was dead. Gone. That's when her mind was worst and they'd send her in for more treatment. And it was on one of these holidays she met God.

'What was he like?'

'How do you imagine he was like?'

I thought about it. She could see my mind working, said: 'That's what he was like, then. As you see him.'

'And what the fuck was he doing in St. Mary's. I mean did he just call in for a cup of tea and a visit.... or what?'

Better it got.

He'd sent The Virgin Mary down to appear in Knock for the second time. When she got to Mayo it was pissing rain and she decided she'd like to go to South America instead. Better weather. New congregation. All that. She sent word to God to tell him her plans. He refused. She threw a tantrum and went drinking. He went down in the Astra to sort it out. Brought a divine Sat/Nav with him. It got him as far as Galway city, then he typed in St. Mary and it picked up the mental home. He got to the door, politely told them he was God and looking for the Virgin Mother and they promptly tackled him to the ground and locked him inside. He'd been there ever since.

'How long ago's that?'

'Ten years.'

'Ten years and no God!'

'Yeah.' She said. 'Fucked up.'

I got thinking about the lads down in Hell. Probably wondering where I'd gone. Wasn't too sure myself.

Kohlia went on.

There'd been a war in Heaven. Blood and torn wings and dead Angels. It was caused by the car. God had wanted to make a symbol of his greatness. Something that "summed it all up." He commissioned one of his mechanics to make the greatest car ever known and soon the Astra was built. A group of Angels got jealous, figuring he'd never use it, and he couldn't drive all that well anyway, so they decided to steal it. They took it for a joyride but soon lost control and crashed it into a big tree. The war started. It went on for centuries. God's side won and he fired them all into Hell.

'And they're there ever since?'

'Yeah. Their only way back is the car. And they know it's in play. And they want it bad. They want to go back and wreck the place.'

'Lovely. So they'll be chasin us?'

'They will. And when they find you, they'll kill you. But that won't matter because if they find the car, they can drive right through the gates of Heaven and we're all dead anyway. Without God, Heaven will tumble in days and the whole Universe will be absorbed into Hell.'

'Where are they, we haven't seen them?'

'God mentioned someone called Tycho, and something about a lake, but I'm a bit hazy on all that.'

'They were talkin about him down below.'

'I think he's human, but he's trying get the car to give it to the dead. He gives people messages for Hell, then kills them so they can bring the information down.'

'So is he workin for Hell, or Hell workin for him?'

'Hell only works for itself, so he's just another pawn.'

'Tell me more about St. Mary's.'

There were people in strait jackets. Others that spent the night screaming. One night, in the bed next to her, a woman set herself on fire and laughed as she burned.

Kohlia and God got talking.

He told her everything. What was happening with the Astra. How he'd met Jennings when he was in for drink, and how we'd come looking for her.

Said he couldn't leave St. Mary's because he had assumed human form, and was subject to human conditions. He'd need the car back to get home to Heaven. He'd parked it outside but it had gotten clamped. Then towed. Then sold to the Lithuanians who sold it to Jennings.

A black spider on the steps. Dogs barking somewhere in the distance. The wheels of a pram rolling by. I put my chin on my elbow and bit lightly on the skin of my arm.

'Why didn't we just break God out when we were in Galway? Why all this messin?'

'Nikki and Dyane?'

'Yeah. But where are they?'

'I don't know. God wouldn't tell me.'

'Why not?'

'It would influence your natural actions. Upset the Chaos.'

'That doesn't surprise me at all.'

'I think it was that he didn't know.'

'How could he not know?'

'When he was God he could predict everything that happened. No, "predict" is the wrong word. It's more like he could see every possible outcome. But now, all stoned and locked up, he can only see so far ahead. His omnipotence is neutralized. Imagine it's a book with ten crucial pages missing in the middle. You need to fill in the blanks. You need to find them. And you need the car until then. I presume it all connects beautifully. Or it doesn't. Either way. Same predicament: The car needs to go back to God and then God needs to drive back to Heaven. Finding Nikki and Dyane is somehow important to that process. Right now, nobody knows how, not even the Almighty, so everything is up to you....'

'No pressure there at all, sure.'

'It's why he told Kurt how to find me, so I'd meet you. Here. And tell you this. This is as far as God predicted. It was the last outcome he could properly see...I meet you. Am reunited with Kurt. And the rest is....up to Chaos.'

'What do *you* think is goin to happen?'

'There's always multiple outcomes that exist at the same time. Us here. Something else happening somewhere else. Connected by invisible threads called *strings*. They form a narrative that we can't see. We can sense it. But we can't see it. It's like excitement. And I'm really excited, but terrified too. If you can feel something, you're still alive. Even if it's fear. But in a world absorbed by Hell....there'll be nothing at all. Not even light. Everything will be sucked into a big crunching city of black ruination.'

Beat. We let that settle. Eventually I said: 'He felt afraid.'

'Who? God?'

'Jennings.'

'Kurt?'

'Yeah, I can see the scene.'

'How?'

'I don't know. He told us about the night he was here and...'
'Oh...'
'I can see him leavin, how he felt. He couldn't handle you.'
'You didn't know either of us back then.'
'Yeah, but me sittin here with you now, I know you'd consume a man. Take everythin he has, become everythin he wants. He'd have to surrender himself completely and that scared him.'
'I hope he's gotten over it.'
'Yeah, I think so. He's a bit of a mess, though.'
'I don't care. I just want to see him. I want my life to finally begin.'
Beat.
'How we gettin back down there, anyway? I mean, do we have to bungee jump off some fuckin... half built church somewhere or somethin...'
She laughed, the world smiled with her. It felt good. Then she said: 'No, you silly dickhead. We take these.'
She took out two capsules. They were black. 'These'll knock us out and we'll wake up there. God and I made them from our meds. He knew the formula. I brought them home. Directions were, when I meet you, we take one each and then we wake up in Hell.'
She handed me one. It was hard, like a marble. Small like a large peanut. I looked up, her eyes dancing like exotic fish at the bottom of a clear blue lake. She asked: 'Ready for a bad trip?'
'You're fuckin cracked.'
She took up the glass of water. 'So I've been told.'

*He was a Nowhereman.*

The pills were made from a mixture of Prozac, Librium, Morphine, Oxycontin, and a dose of something The Almighty himself had introduced. It left a metallic taste on my tongue as I swallowed. Kohlia waited for a reaction, an effect, something like that. Nothing came. Then she took hers, and sat back. We watched each other, like we'd just taken Acid for the first time and didn't know what to expect. Feeling kinda nervous, I asked: 'What now?'

'We wait.'

'How long's it take?'

'God said about ten minutes.'

'How's it supposed to feel?'

'Strange.'

'I figured that, but...'

'I've never been to Hell before. You have.'

'It's kinda like you'd expect.' Pause. 'Where are we anyway, like where's this house...?'

She looked around, like it was all new to her. At the door, at the porch. Then the garden. 'Galway. Renmore. I don't like it.'

'Looks alright.'

'I'm going to see Kurt again, amn't I?'

'Yeah, how d'ya feel?'

'Anxious. Scared. Curious.'

'Did you really love him?'

'Yes.'

'How come?'

'How come anything?'

She looked at my knee, her eyes thinking back. Blue oceans. Dancing stars. I was feeling tired. There was a smell like old paint. She went. 'Maybe it was his mind.'

'He's a lush now, though. I mean, he's...'

'I don't want to know...Jack.'

'Did your parents ever get over it?'

'No. We just had an argument about it.'

'I think we heard some of that. It was goin on downstairs before I met you in the bathroom.'

'It's probably a loop that's playing in the ether, like a moment that can't find its way forward.'

'Yeah, my thoughts exactly. A loop. Whatever the fuck that is.'

She smiled. I asked. 'You an only child?'

'Yeah. Why?'

'Just wonderin if you've got any sisters.'

'For you? Sorry. No. You?'

'Yeah, only child too.'

'Weird isn't it? Like...lonely.'

'I don't think about it much'

'How are you feeling?'

'The tips of my fingers are startin to tingle.'

'Mine too. Can I sit closer to you?'

'Go ahead.'

She did. It made me shake. I went 'Was there anyone else?'

'What d'you mean?'

'You're a young girl, younger when you fell for Jennings...'

'Another man...?'

'Yeah.'

Her hair was dry now. Black and thin. She said: 'There was one guy in St. Mary's. He was crazy though.'

'Figure that.'

'We used to fuck in the caretakers storeroom at night.'

'What was he in for?'

'Schizo. Can you see the long halls?'

I tried. Saw them. Long and dark. A smell of disinfectant. Moonlight across a marble floor. 'Think I have it.'

'I used to love that moonlight. I don't know why. Can you smell the food in the afternoons?'

'The cheesy cabbage smell?'

'Yeah, it always reminds me of him.'

'Where's he now?'

'It doesn't matter.'

'It was only natural I s'pose.'

In the sky, the sun darkened. She went: 'That's what God said.'

'I'll have to remember that.'

'He was a Nowhereman.'

'What's a Nowhereman?'

She said: 'You don't know?'

'No.'

Beat

'Things are going to happen when we leave here.'

'Like what? Will we have to reverse the car up Croagh Patrick or somethin and find some secret passageway into a room full of tormented saints that starved themselves so bad they ate their Rosary beads...?'

She laughed again. But the trees lost their shine. 'You're very entertaining.'

'I've been compared to God.' She laughed more. I said. 'So what else is goin to happen?'

'A paradoxical explosion.'

'Huh?'

'There's three universes at work here. The first one is Hell. The second one is where me and Kurt lived before. And then there's this one – the present. When we meet Kurt all three will collide and there'll be a collapse. Two universes will cease to exist...or at least....they'll stop having an influence on the others.'

Her soft voice, almost a slur. 'I'm getting a bit dizzy.' She leaned closer. 'Are you?'

I checked. I wasn't. But my brain felt like it was getting bigger, as if it wanted to crack outta my skull. I told her. She said: 'Hope we got the formula right.'

'What's the chances ye got it wrong?'

'Slim. Did you love Dyane?'

'Yeah. I think so.'

She lay on my knee. It felt good. Summer teenage twilight good. Fuckin brilliant. She held my hand. It was soft. It felt like there was a terrible weight over our heads. Her voice slurring more, she went. 'Why are we going to Hell, Jack?'

'I don't know. I don't know anythin anymore.'

The porch became uncomfortable. I wanted to stand up but couldn't. I put my hand on her head, let her hair fall through my fingers. Smooth skin on her soft neck. She said: 'Keep talking about normal stuff. Keep going...I'm getting afraid....'

Something gripped me around the chest. Legs like pillars of concrete. 'What's your favourite song?'

'*Strange Boat.* By *The Waterboys.*'

'What about *Fisherman's Blues?*'

'Have you listened to it?'

'Just heard a busker sing it one night.'

'How's the Astra?'

'Flyin it.'

Heavy arms. I said: 'This must be what it's like to die.'

'That's not the kind of normal talking I'm looking for right now....'

The sounds of life faded, like the echo of bells far away. She put her hand on my knee, rubbed it for a second. 'Thanks, Jack.'

'For what?'

'Coming to save me.'

'I'm just rollin with it.'

'You've made me feel sane for the first time in a long while...'

Then, the feeling you get when you're on a train, with your back to the driver, and it takes off and there's a surge.

Couldn't breathe.

Rush of air.

She held me tight, squeezing her fingers into my palm, like we were in a plane that was crashing. There were flashes. Childhood. Random things. Pain in my heart like it was about to burst. Kohlia screamed: 'Jack!'

But I couldn't see her, feel her, nothing.

Then.

We were back in Kohlia's room. On the bed. Facing each other. It was a divine gift. To open your eyes and she's the first thing you see. She looked a bit shook, said: 'So this is Hell?'

'Here at last.'

'Maybe *I am* crazy.'

'What's real is real.'

She leaned over and kissed me. The walls frowned. The night outside was angry. I said: 'Let's go.'

We walked down the stairs. There was silence and dead air and broken plaster on the ground and a shaking rumble somewhere in the distance. I already missed everything about the real world.

The lads were arguing. 'Where the fuck is he?' Said Chris.

'How do I know?' Replies Jennings. 'He went upstairs for a piss. Maybe they killed him.'

'Who's "they"?'

'I don't know. Whoever was up there when he left. Let me think. What's that noise?'

'What noise?'

'There's a thumpin somewhere.'

'I don't know. A marchin fuckin army of dead trolls or somethin. What're we goin to do?'

'I'm thinkin!'

'How's that goin?'

'Not great.'

'Lovely. Maybe we should just go?'

'Where?'

'Get the car and leave.'

Jennings thinks and says: 'No. He needs the car. We *all* need the car.'

I walked in. Said: 'It's ok. I'm back.'

Chris said: 'Where the fuck were you?'

Kohlia walked in then with: 'Hello.'

This caused a stir. Jennings said: 'Fuckin hell.'

She said: 'I know.'

And then everything exploded.

*Be here all day otherwise.*


Woke up feeling timber and tired, like I'd spent the whole day before picking stones. The back of my head was damp. Dry eyes, cracked lips. Thought about Kohlia and I wanted a drink. *Harvey Wallbanger.* Figure that. It was days later and we were sleeping in the car somewhere on the fringes of Hell. After the explosion, we'd woken up on the ground and everything was wrecked. The house had disintegrated, big crater on the ground. Nothing left except us and the Astra. So we'd sat in and got going. Somehow we'd found the desert road again and it hadn't changed. Same sand and the long grey snake of lonely miles.

I got up and walked outside and there was a smell of burnt straw and the sun sprayed light over the scorched distance. Some rays bounced off the Astra and it felt good, like assurance. Put my hands in my pockets. Felt the square box of a safe twenty Benson and lit one up.

Something moved at my feet. It was an insect, like an ant. First time I saw life in this place, other than us. I shivered and exhaled. It hovered like a ghost. I watched it dissipate. I'd dreamt about her last night, Dyane. The memory fading, same as the smoke. Tried to hold it but it went away like a dying distance.

Dragged hard. Finished it and lit another. Movement in the background. It was Chris, looking tired and cold. 'You have a spare one of them?'

The dream was gone, left a lingering something, serene and soft. Then it expired. I gave him the cigarette. We let the silence roll. Then he said: 'So whaddy'a think?'

'I don't know. Keep goin I suppose.'

My mouth was still dry, like I'd been licking a camel's hole all night. We got in and started driving. After a while, Chris said: 'Do you think they survived?'

'Jennings and Kohlia?'

'Yeah.'

'Who knows anythin anymore in this place?'

'You worried about Dyane?'

'Naturally.'

'I can't believe God's in the mental.'

'That's what Kohlia reckoned anyway.'

A sign appeared in the distance. I hit the brakes when it got closer. It was a huge billboard that said:

Bambino Highway
Next Left.

I drove on, asked: 'What'll we do?'

'It's the first sign we've seen in thousands of miles,' said Chris. 'I think we should take it.'

'What do you think a *Bambino* is?'

'Haven't a fuck's clue.'

Midnight Oil, *Beds are Burning*, in my head. We got to the turn and I indicated and drove. Same story. Long road. Sahara scene either side. Silence.

Then. Something like shadows materialized. Chris took up the twenty Benson and lit one. After, he threw me the box and I sparked up. The shadows came closer. Solitary tress appeared in the dead landscape either side. Small shoots of grass. A light wind, like oxygen in a stagnant cave. Another big billboard appeared from nowhere saying:

*Paddy's Bar.*
**Ten minute drive at the speed of light.**
**Free Coffee for the driver.**

Beneath was a picture of a fuel pump. A knife and fork. And a pint.

I said: 'Looks promisin.'

'I'd love a rasher sandwich.'

'I want my free coffee. We goin at the speed light?'

'Not unless she's in fifth. Remember the roundabout?'

'Oh yeah.'

'Will I hit it?'

'Be here all day otherwise.'
'Sound, better fuck on the seatbelts.'
We did. I revved. The Astra collected all its pistons and got ready for the surge. We peaked on fourth at 50,000 M/ph and then I hit it.

Moist lips. Long afternoons. Warmth and Vulva.

### *Fuck this... Joe?!*

Things were lush now. A few ponds. Less desert. Thin road. *Paddy's* was a thatched cottage and a pub. Chris said: 'Better park the car somewhere safe in case.'

Discovered a small gate into a big field. I squeezed it in and made sure it was out of sight behind some bushes.

Then we got out and walked back. There was a light wind and the sound of water. It was still possible to see the desert in the distance, a yellow sea of sand and empty, but standing on gravel was good and familiar.

*Paddy's* had a bright red door and petrol pumps to the right. There was movement inside. 'We better knock, anyway.' Said Chris.

He did. The door opened. There was nobody there. It just squealed inwards.

So we walked in.

Interior. Counter. A smell like sawdust and coal. Couple of geriatrics working on some *Guinness* and whisky chasers. Calm light on their heads. No hurry on them. Fire going. Fella behind the bar with a goatee gave us a look, said: 'Lads.'

Chris answered: 'Are ye well?'

The old men grunted. Bar man asked: 'Pints all round?'

I said: 'Sound.'

The drinks came. Chris said: 'Fine spot.'

Barman extended his hand. 'I'm Joe.'

We did the intro. He asked: 'Are ye lost or what?'

Told him we kinda were and we kinda weren't. Wasn't too sure if we could trust him or not. Then he said: 'Well ye came at the right time, anyway.'

Chris took a long drink, asked: 'Why's that?'

He pointed to a big banner that said: "Happy Birthday, Nola!"

'Savage party planned here tonight.'

'Oh yeah?'

He was about to talk more when the bolt on the door rattled and the hinges creaked and this ride walked in. Sallow skin. Huge brown eyes. Black top and tight jeans. Hair autumnal. Joe greeted her. She had an accent. South American. She eyed us up. Chris stared at her chest. She let it slide. We talked. She said what Joe had said. 'You come at a good time. I'm Melissa.' She said it like this: *Mallissa.*

We shook hands. Then she leaned in and kissed me twice on the cheek. Smelled like caramel. Chris asked: 'What time's this party startin?'

'Soon. You should join.'

'We will.'

'Ok.'

'Ok.'

'Ok. Ciao.'

There was mischief in her eyes. The foreign kind, like she knows well what you're thinking and she's going to fuck with you for a while. Her boots echoed away and she started organizing tables in the back. I asked Joe: 'Where's she from?'

And he said: 'Here.'

'Where's here?'

'Ye don't know?'

'No.'

'Ye're in for a bit of learnin tonight, so.'

He went out back. I said to Chris: 'What'll we do?'

He shrugged. 'Place seems alright. Be no harm to have a few pints and see what happens. The women might even be here somewhere.'

'Fair point.'

'Better than bein on the road all fuckin day too....'

Pints later. We were too bushted to drive. Joe told us not to worry. We'd be sound for a place to stay and were we not staying for the party anyway?

So we ordered another round and then the crowd came.

A real mental crew. Guitars. Sombreros. Bongos. Already sorta pissed. The place exploded with their arrival and they didn't waste any time kicking off their music. It was in a language we didn't understand. Same kind of accent as Melissa. Soon the place was packed and warm.

We drank more. A blonde woman came round with a basket of cocktail sausages and chips. We wired into them. Later she came back with chicken nuggets and I ate the whole lot myself.

There was a mouthwatering smell of fat being cooked. Someone said they were frying steaks out by the back bar. We picked up the pints and bursthed out. There was a small lowering of noise in the crowd, like they were afraid we might be Travellers. Melissa came and saved us. Told us to take a seat. We did. The band played on. There was an air of excitement. It was all about waiting for Nola, whoever the fuck she was. Suddenly there was an almighty uproar of delighted screaming and she was here.

Out came the cake. Lots of candles. Singing. Photographs.

Got on to *Jaggerbombs*.

After four of them, I thought I knew all there was to know about dancing.

Tried to tear it up and nearly killed Joe with a stray elbow. 'Relax!!' He said.

*Butterballs. Baby Guinness.* Swinging young ones around. Eventually Nola caught me at the bar, said: 'Thanks for coming, but I don't know who you are?'

She was blonde, up to my shoulder, all heart. I told her roughly. She shouted over the music: 'Joe said something about that. Are you looking for the Bambino Highway?'

'Yeah, I think so. I don't even know. Wherever the hell Dyane and Nikki are gone, we'll go there.'

'Is that your car hidden outside?'

'The Astra? Yeah.'

'Where'd you get it?'

'Fella called Jennings bought it on *DoneDeal* in Galway.'

'Galway?!'

'Yeah. Off a couple of Lithuanians.'

'You and I will need to sit down tomorrow, ok?'

'Ok.'

'We need to talk about that car. And Dyane. And where you're going.'

'Sound.'

'I can't do it tonight, because of the party....'

'Jesus, don't worry about it...'

'But I think we've been waiting for you.'

'How d'ya mean?'

'Tomorrow, tomorrow. Let's do a shot.'

'Here I'll get them. Two double *Jaggerbombs*, Joe, when you get a chance, good man.'

They came. We drank. It was highly potent. Fuckin dynamite. She said: 'Do you like the music?'

'Be better if I knew what they were singin.'

'Oh you don't know?'

'No.'

'It's an ancient musical dialect. Listen hard. You'll get it.' She kissed me on the cheek, then pointed a finger. 'Enjoy yourself. Don't forget. Tomorrow. Serious talk.'

The night went on. Someone handed me a dinner of steak and potatoes and I lashed into it with serious purpose. Washed it down with a can of *Bulmers*. Started wondering about Chris. Hadn't seen him in a while. Then Melissa arrived beside me and there was a blank.

Now we're all sitting around a table and the band have finished. Some people are singing old songs. Melissa is sitting on my knee. One of the musicians still has his guitar and everyone wants him to sing. He eventually does. Has a haunting, coarse voice. High vocals at the end. It's the kinda moment that hangs delicate in the balance. Requires absolute silence for full appreciation and effect. Nobody dared talk. Take a drink. Or even move. He had his eyes closed. Feeling it. Living it. That vibe.

He was about half way through when Chris fell in the door. It was like he was trying to take it off the hinges. Thish, rump; arackle: Whang! Rumpa thump rump. Muttering: "...fuckin bastardin cunt of a fuckin door...."

Wide eyes. Frantic. Hair standing on his head. He almost knocked a stool but caught it awkwardly and tried to stand it up straight. Everyone looked at him like he was mad. He asked: 'Is the party over?!'

The silence gave him the answer and he said: 'Fuck! And is the bar closed?'

He looked around and realized it was and said. 'Shite! I went to the car for a joint and fell asleep.'

The singer left the guitar down. The moment's over. Everyone's annoyed but no one says anything. Melissa turns and asks. 'You have a car?'

I said: 'Yeah, Opel Astra, 1994. Besht fuckin car in the world.'

Her eyes went wide. 'Silver?' She asked.

'Yeah.'

Everyone at the table stopped what they were doing. Chris asked: 'Where the fuck is Joe gone anyway?'

The musician turned to me. 'It's impolite to make jokes like that. You are messing with a concept that is very important to us.'

'Sure what am I jokin about?'

'You say you have a Silver Opel Astra. 1994? That's impossible.'

Chris was wandering from the front bar to the back with: 'Fuck this.... Joe!'

I said: 'I have yeah, it's outside sure.'

Nola intervened. 'I talked to him about it, Greg. We're not sure. We're going to see it tomorrow.'

'Tomorrow?!' He said. 'What's tomorrow?! Why not now? If the car is there....'

'Tomorrow. Now is not the time.'

'We've been waiting this long, why wait more?'

'Because we need to be sure. We can't send them driving into the....'

'*Now's* the time, Nola!'

There was the makings of an argument out back. Chris was mumbling to a woman who was telling him to leave. A baby began to cry and the woman lost her temper and tore into Chris with vicious abuse. Nola said: 'Oh, he's woken the child.'

Melissa took my hand. 'Come with me.'

'Where?'

'Now.'

Greg stood up. 'I can't believe this.'

And left. A general tumult erupted. Jackets retrieved. Chinking glasses. Drip trays clattering. We got outside. Melissa's body. Delighted cold air. I was feeling lucky. She looked at the car. 'Is this it?'

'Yeah.'

'We will drive to my house.'

'What about Chris?'

'He'll be fine. Come to my place.'

So we went to her place.

*She's a ride, but, pity she's mental.*

She lived up a mountain. Drive took half an hour. Hard to concentrate when you're full of sauce. Windy roads with no walls. You drive off and that's the end of you, a sharp loud fall into a dark scrubby nowhere. Then there was the obstacles. We had to stop three times to hunt the sleeping sheep out of the way. Melissa was mostly thoughtful. Now and then she'd do something. Caress the dashboard, turn a knob on the heating or look into the empty back seat. Her strong scent floated around the car. You could almost touch it. I was drowsy after a while, had to drive with one eye closed. She didn't notice and we somehow made it.

At her place. Stonewashed walls. Bright wood on the windows. Big hill. Revved too hard and put stones flying everywhere. Almost hit the gable of the house but skidded to a stop just in time. Got out. Unsteady. Dodged a puke by swallowing hard then I fell towards the wooden front door. Light breeze. Smell of a smoking tyre. Melissa screamed: 'The car!'

I looked back. The Astra was out of gear. Handbrake off. Rolling down backwards. Fuck! Ran after it. Wonky legs. There was a loud crunching sound. Then a crash and the muted sound of breaking glass. The indicator was broke. Bits of red shrapnel on her driveway. Cuntish. Sat in and drove it back up and made sure it was in gear this time.

'Idiot!' She said.

We got into the house. Snug interior. Lots of tea cosys and rocking chairs and rugs. She gave me something to drink. It was small and strong and sobered me up in seconds. Reality came fast, like the click of a photograph.

Then. We talked all night. On her soft bed. Til the sun came up and sent shafts of solar light through her large window. Her room smelled of flowers I couldn't name. She told me lots of things. Her voice like Spanish love poetry. All affection. She told me how she grew up in Peru. How they got their summer holidays at Christmas. How she met a fella and left against her parent's wishes. He was big into drugs and she tried them an odd time herself. They moved to Bilbao, in Spain. She worked as a waitress. He was always playing around with other women. She caught him at it. They fought. He threw her out. She couldn't go home – fear and shame. She roamed Europe. Got homeless. Fell in with a bad crowd. Ended up using needles, then turning tricks. Found God when she had a child. The child died but she wouldn't tell me how. A look of intense pain flashed across her face with the memory. I didn't push it. And now she was here. Waiting to be let go.

Let go from where?

She knew all about the war in Heaven and God being in the mental. There was a prophecy. One day a great car would come from the north. The Silver Opel Astra, 1994. It would be the first sign that God was to be released from St. Mary's. The Astra was the only car capable of traversing the Bambino Highway. Some said it was a myth. Others a legend. More still swore it to be true. There'd been false dawns before. A Ford Focus last year. A Vauxhall Cavalier the year before. But never an Astra. This is why she was excited. This was the prophecy. The car would be returning to God and they'd all be released

Her big eyes. Warm breath. Time doesn't exist here, she said. One year in the normal world was worth a thousand to them. They never grew old. Only more cynical that they'll never be saved. Cynical until now. Until we arrived. She wanted to see her child again. We were the hope. This was why she wanted to make sure. Why she brought me home. And now she was convinced.

I said: 'So where exactly are we right now?'

'I don't know.' She said. 'Some of us think it's purgatory or some kind of limbo. The truth is, we have no idea. We died and we woke up here and we've been waiting for the car ever since.'

'What's the Bambino highway?'

'It's the lake. Behind *Paddy's*. All we know for sure is that you need to get over the lake and return the Astra to God. That'll set off another train of events and then we all get...' She struggled for the word, then said: '...processed.'

'What kind of a train of events?'

'You'll need to talk to Nola.'

'Why?'

'Because she knows….things. She's our spiritual leader. Once she confirms everything we'll talk about what you're supposed to do…'

'Are we supposed to *do* somethin?'

'Of course. Why else would you be here?'

'To find Dyane. And Nikki.'

'They're just motivations. Triggers. The whole of existence is more important.'

'Does it not bother you, all that about God?'

'It terrifies me. But you're here. So the prophecy is coming true.'

I tried to think of more questions. The only one I could come up with was: 'Will it matter now that I broke an indicator?'

'No.'

'Why?'

'Tom will fix it.'

'Who's Tom?'

'You'll see.'

'So you reckon…'

'Yes, you are the saviours.'

'And what do we do?'

'You drive the car over the highway.'

'Sometimes you call it a Highway, others a lake, why?'

'Cos the Highway is the lake. You'll be driving over water.'

I thought to myself. "She's a ride, but, pity she's mental." Then I asked: 'And what happens after that?'

She blinked and shrugged and said: 'That's all I know. We're stuck here until then. We're all supposed to be in Heaven, but the gates are closed because God is…ill…so this is like a…how do you say…a traffic jam.'

Silence. She put her hand on mine. It was warm. I touched her face and kissed her. She responded. We sailed a dark calm water, strong rhythms. Then I slept a thousand deaths.

*Calm accentuated.*

Woke up and she was standing over me, holding a cup of tea. 'Time to go.' She said.

I got dressed. Let the body settle. Calm accentuated. Sat on the edge of the bed. Took my watch off the bedside locker. The time had stopped. Music started downstairs. That same language. An echoing lament, electric guitar. Slow beats.

Shoes. Laces. Thinking. Stairs. More echoes. Smell of something brewing, like punch. I went toward it. She was there. Looking out the window. Taking in the song. She was like a statue, entranced in the tune. Blue Jeans. Sandals. I knew twas an image I'd never forget. She noticed me and broke the silence, with: 'You've heard this song before.'

I wasn't sure if it was a question. 'No. What's it called?'

'*Opio*. It's from *Heroes de Silencio*.'

'Why don't I understand what they're sayin?'

'Because it's the language of the soul. Our words are too primitive and coarse to describe the emotions.'

She had a point. It was like serotonin acupuncture.

'What about *Fisherman's Blues*?'

'That's not for this part of your journey. You'll know when it's time.'

She took down a book. Opened a page. Pointed at a diagram of two opposing triangles, like an egg timer without the frame. 'This is where you came from. This is where you're going.'

'Right.'

'You see the middle, where the worlds almost touch?'

'I do, yeah.'

She put a brown finger on the apex. Pale long nail. 'We are there. That's the lake.'

'And we drive over it?'

'Yes. But you'll need this music.'

'Why?'

'Because no one is allowed to cross into those waters without playing it. It's like garlic to a vampire. The dead can't touch you once they hear it.' Sleeveless black shirt. Breasts and perfume. 'Once they see the Astra they'll go insane. They're dead and they're bitter. But if you play this song, they won't be able to harm you.'

'How'll the dead see the Astra? Are they watchin us from above?'

'No. They'll be under the water, trying to drag you down.'

'You never mentioned that.'

'I was saving it.'

—

It was time to go back to *Paddy's*. Got sorted and made the way over. Same craic. Long drive. Sheep. Better scenery when it's bright. Lake opposite her house. She asked: 'Have you used the radio yet?'

'In the car? No. We all forgot our Mp3 players.'

'We'll get Tom to hook you up.'

We got to the pub. Chris was sitting outside. Having a smoke. We pulled in and he said: 'Well?'

'How's the head?'

'I'm absolutely fucked. You?'

'Not too bad.'

'Your one inside is after tearin the hole off me.'

'Why?'

'Somethin about wakin a child?'

'Oh yeah. Who's in there anyway?'

'No one really. What's the plan?'

'We're waitin for Nola to come. See how we're fixed then.'

We entered. Dark. Geriatrics gone. Smell of a newly washed floor. Joe behind the bar. He looked at me, then at Melissa, didn't say anything.

Nola arrived with Greg a while later. We sat around the same table as the night before. She opened. 'I've inspected the car. It's true.'

Greg said: 'We want you to leave tonight.'

Chris said: 'Leave for where?'

Nola explained everything Melissa had told me back at the house.

Pause, then Chris said: 'I can't find any positive spin to put on that at all.'

Greg became uneasy. 'I'll take your place if you don't want to go.'

'Shssh...Greg.' Said Nola, 'it has to be these two.'

Joe asked from the bar: 'Ye alright for drinks?'

We told him yeah. Chris said: 'This is mental.'

'It's the only choice we have.' Said Nola.

'I'll do anythin for Nikki, I mean, I want to save her, but you're talkin about drivin a car over water.'

Greg entered: 'It's not just normal waters. It's the purgatorial bath of the dead.'

'Right yeah, whatever, but the fuckin thing might still sink, amn't I right?'

He got agitated. 'Not if you have faith.'

'Faith in what? I can't swim for shite.'

'The car won't sink.'

'Why not?'

'Why do you think, genius?'

We all went quiet. I mentioned the indicator. Greg called me a clown.

Then Nola asked Joe to get Tom.

Tom arrived. Tall. Black hair. Suspicious. He said: 'I seen the car outside. I didn't believe it til then. I thought ye were talkin shite.'

'Can you fix it?'

He looked at the ground. 'I'll take a look. Where's the keys?'

I gave him the keys. He left.

Chris said: 'Tell me this. When all this is said and done, and we drive over the lake, assumin we survive, where do we even end up?'

'Galway.' Said Nikki.

'Just like that?'

'You'll need to bring the car to St. Mary's and make sure God gets it. When you save God, you'll return to the point when Nikki and Dyane disappeared. Jack will wake up beside Dyane and you beside Nikki and it'll be like none of this ever happened.'

'Like a dream?'

'As opposed to the nightmare of failure, yes. The tear in the time-space continuum will repair itself at the point where it broke, as in, where they disappeared. There'll be others lookin for the car when you return.'

'Like who?' Asked Chris.

'There's a satanic group in Galway called *The Red Dragons*.... have you heard of them?'

'No.'

'They're run by a man called Tycho.'

'Someone mentioned him back the road...Frank, the fella that killed his wife with a lump hammer.'

Greg sighed. Nola continued. 'Tycho made contact with the dead during a Black Mass a year ago. They're using him to track down the car in Galway. Luckily, you're here so he can't find you. But equally as unlucky, you need to drive back through the dead lake, where you could be killed, drowned, dragged into the fires of Hell, or just tortured for their own amusement. Either way, it'll mean they have the car and the race is over and we're all....dust.'

'Still,' said Chris. 'I don't understand why we're even here... how does this connect to Nikki and Dyane...?'

'There's only one thing that can get God out of St. Mary's and you need to bring it back to him. *That's* why you're here. You needed to get the car to us. And you wouldn't have come if you weren't searching for Nikki and Dyane.'

'But the car could have been used by anyone.' Said Chris. 'It's been ten years. Why us? Now? A fuckin decade later!'

'When Jack took John Hanover's job it put everything in motion.' Said Nikki. 'Meeting Jennings meant you'd use the car and meet Kohlia and eventually end up here, where you'll pick up what you need to give to God. I don't know why it took ten years, but, here we are...'

I said: 'It was clamped outside St. Mary's. Then towed and sold to a couple of Lithuanians. They sold it to Jennings and he locked it up until he met us and we drove it here.'

Everyone stared at me until I said: 'Kohlia told me. I met her a few days back. And God told her. That was as far as he could predict....or somethin....'

'Jack,' Said Nola. 'I want to talk to you alone. Come with me.'

*We'll starve, but not before we burn.*

We walked out the back door. There was a porch. Then a garden. Grass. Small trees. Nola said: 'I wish you'd told me you met Kohlia.'

'You *know* her?'

'Yes.'

'She never said.'

'She probably didn't want to interrupt the Chaos.'

'Fuck the Chaos. And how do *you* know so much about it all?'

'I was an Angel.'

'So what're you doin here?'

'It's a long story. The road you came from is destroyed. We send out scouts every week. The desert is growing by thousands of miles each day. There's no way back. Over the lake is the only way out of here.'

'And what if we tell ye to go fuck yourselves.'

'Then everything is lost.'

I looked at the water. Small ripples. Reflection of the sky. Lots of distance. 'Lost?'

'Don't think it'll be easy, Jack. If you fail, then no one is ever released. Our trees here will wilt and wither. The gravel will disappear. The sun will get hotter. We'll starve, but not before we burn. The desert will keep expanding and overcome us. You've seen it. All the arid sand and no life? It's the dying heart of this place.'

'All I'm lookin for is a girl called Dyane.'

'And you'll find her.'

'Where?'

She pointed to the water. 'Over there. Beyond that. Everyone here is depending on you.'

'For what?'

'Everything.'

She looked at the ground, at her feet, painted toes. Her hair moved a bit. White top. Necklace. She said: 'If you stay, you'll die here with all the rest of us. If you go, I don't know what happens, but at least there's a chance.'

'Melissa said to talk to you about what we're supposed to do....it's not all just about Nikki and Dyane....what's this thing we need to bring back to God?'

We were interrupted by Tom. He pushed through the trees, said: 'Sorry.'

'What?'

'It's about the car. I can fix the indicator, but the Aquaflux is fucked and she'll need new speakers.'

'How long will that take?'

'Few days, besht part of a week.'

I looked at Nola. She folded her arms and looked at the stones. 'That's ok,' she said. 'Maybe it's for the best.'

I asked: 'What's an Aquaflux?'

'It's to stop the car from sinking.' Said Nola.

'Oh, I thought we were just goin to wing it. On faith alone?'

And Tom looked at me like I was mad.

*There's a lot ridin on ye.*

'You'll be sound,' said Tom. 'So long as you have the Aquaflux.'

About that: The Aquaflux would create a ballast under the Astra to prevent us from sinking. Only "Astras" were capable of having the Aquaflux installed, it was to do with the unique style of the engine and the car's inherent resilience to negative conditions. This is what Tom told me when I went with him after talking to Nola.

We were a couple of miles up the road from *Paddy's*. You could tell he was a natural with cars.

'Only one other car can compare to the Astra,' He said. Overalls. Wrench in his hand. Twisted something. 'Hasn't been seen for a long time, though. American make, Omni, Dodge.'

'Oh yeah?'

'Yeah, girl in Chicago owned the last known model. Took good care of it too, but they say the devils got it and now it's in pieces somewhere. They were tryin to clone the Astra but they made a shite of it.'

'So where does this flux yoke go then, or what?'

We sat in. He smelled like motor oil. Pointed at the gearbox. 'See, I'm going to have to come up from underneath, probably put her over a pit or somethin, and get right inside the carburetor to install it. It's the best place. Direct access to the gears. It'll be like a second motor. Spinnin so fast that it'll keep the water out and enough pressure under the car to keep ye floatin, like a hovercraft kinda.'

'Did the Omni Dodge have one, too?'

'No. Transmission ya see. Once she's manual you can fit her in easy, diddle around. You have a box like in the Dodge, then you have ta take the whole thing out, mess around with all them cogs and coils, then hope it works. It's a great car, but the Astra, well you know, it's just an Astra, and this is *thee* Astra so I don't want any gears slippin on ye when you're out there.'

He put his hand round the top of the gear stick. Pushed it back and over. Rudder dudder. Rudder. 'How ye feelin about it?'

'I don't know.'

'There's a lot ridin on ye.'

'You sure we'll make it?'

'With a baby like this, I don't see why not.'

The car shook for a second in a strong breeze. Tom looked up, out the window. His eyes danced with a thought. 'Some breeze...'

'Breeze?'

'We don't get much wind ya see. Only been kinda comin since ye lads arrived.'

'Wasn't there somethin about music, too?'

'Yeah.' He pointed at the radio, stuck his finger into the tape deck. 'I'm goin to hook you up to this. You'll have an Mp3 player. Sony. I prefer them to I-pods and they're more reliable... there's a lot of shite on it but it'll get ye through....'

Silence. Then he asked: 'Did you always know?'

'What?'

'That you were destined for this?'

'To help God out of a mental home? No. And I still don't.'

'But ye're here all the same.'

'We are.'

'Fair fucks to ye. Ye'll meet Nola's fella on the far side too.'

'Of the lake?'

'Yeah.'

'Who's he?'

'He's waitin there. You'll know him when ye see him. Did she not say anythin about him?'

'No. I don't even know what we're supposed to do. Why we're even really here.'

'You should ask Melissa about the plants.'

'The plants?'

'Yeah. The plants. Better get workin on this yoke.'

He turned the ignition. The engine started. 'Here, I'll throw you back....'

*The plants.*

Tom worked like fuck on the car. I spent most of the time with Melissa. We sat through longs dusks. She showed me the world with a wave of her hand. The lakes and the green fields and the mountains. The country air and the serenity. The scraggy hilltops and blue skies and then beyond to the encroaching yellow desert. We smoked together for hours. She compared it to Peru. And the north of Spain. We talked about the Basques and the Incas. National identity. Her father. My family. People in her town. People in mine and how the world isn't all that different no matter where you go. She told me that a bright blue sky is the land of the unborn, where they hover in innocence, waiting to be allowed in, and the night stars are the glimmering Halos in the supreme Heaven. And how most of the people in this oasis are decent. They don't wander out much. Devout types. Most of them had refused to come to the party because they were afraid to enjoy themselves. We talked about everything but the coming departure and the intensity that had come between us and the confusion caused by our solitary time together. I thought of Jennings and how he must have felt when Kohlia left and how part of him died with her leaving. I missed Dyane too, but I didn't want to think about it. Eventually she asked: 'Are you ready to know why you're really here?'

—

She brought us to a forest the next day. I was driving. She was in the front. Chris in the back. We pulled in and got out. It was raining. There were trees. Tall, taller, and massive entirely. The leaves were the size of a car. The trunks the width of a council house. Looked like they grew straight into the bluish sky above. There was the smell of a greenhouse. Things moved inside. Branches, animals, all that. We let the silence fall. Asked her to explain. Something cracked in the distance, like a branch breaking. More rain. I was cold, like a dreary wet Wednesday evening in Ballinrobe. She looked up and said. 'Come inside.'

Wood life crunched under our feet. Sap on the large barks. A smell like glue. Everything was bright green. When the drops fell, they were heavy and landed with a splash. Melissa put her hand on the nearest tree, caressed it with affection, like it was a horse. I knelt down and picked up a twig. My hands felt huge. The twig was strong, and wet too. The moisture glistened. Insects ran around the leaves on the ground. Everything seemed amplified, like your ears have popped on a flight.

The oxygen around the trees was pure, blow the head of ya. Melissa was part of the life of the place. An important element in the local ecology. Some sort of essential ingredient. There were plants. All colours. Not like any I'd ever seen. A smell like a funeral in November. The air whispered soft things. The damp got on to my back, soaked in. I was freezing. Dew on my forehead. Brain took a speed wobble. I thought of coming round the roundabout. A return to the point of conception. The meaning of death.

Found a fallen log. It was perfect for sitting on. Took a seat and Melissa pulled up some plants and said: 'Mimosa Hostilis.'

'Like Champagne and Orange juice?' Asked Chris.

'No. More like Magic Mushrooms.'

'Psilocybin.' Said Chris. I looked at him. He shrugged. 'That's the chemical in Magic Mushrooms.'

'But that's not what's in these.' Said Melissa.

I took one of them in my hand. It was rich in texture. Felt like nettles that didn't sting, or wet paint that doesn't come off on your fingers.

'We need to make a fire.' She said.

We used branches and matches and leaves. Took a while to get it going.

'The plant reacts with DMT or Dimethtyltryptamine in the brain. It comes from the Pineal gland.' She said. 'Mushrooms are different. DMT is a naturally occurring chemical in the body. It helps with the sleep cycles and can create euphoric feelings, but it needs to be infused with certain plants to have a lasting effect.' She picked up the plants. 'Such as Mimosa Hostilis. When it's all together it forms a tea called Ayahuasca. It's used in Shamanic rituals and other ancient practices.' She was putting stones by the flames. Making sure they got some heat. 'It's how the Shamans reach supreme states of consciousness. Other realities. It's thought our consciousness is an inferior state of existence, that there are purer undiluted versions out there. We just don't know it. Until we take DMT. We'll need water. Get the pot I brought, it's in the car.'

I got it and filled some water from a large leaf, then put it on the fire to boil. Chris said: 'Wasn't there somethin like this called The Spirit Molecule?'

He lit a Benson. Glowing.

'Yes.' She said. 'A man called Strassman, biological psychiatrist, was researching it. He wanted to know the biological triggers for Spiritual Experiences. But DMT is more like the spiritual cause of biological episodes....' She looked at it. 'We boil it up. It reacts with the enzymes inside us. Creates a surplus from the pineal gland and reaches the brain before the body has a chance to metabolise it...typically it's a ten to fifteen minute trip....'

She put them into the water, added something from a bottle and some other seeds and cloves. When it was all ready she filled three cups. They were hot and we had to keep switching hands. The stuff itself smelled like watery soup and incense and burning plastic. We all looked at each other. I thought about Kohlia. And the trip I'd had with her. Musta been something similar. It was ready.

'This is the stuff you need to give God.' Said Melissa. 'You can find less potent mixtures in Galway but this is the necessary recipe to get him out. I'll prepare it in a special bottle to bring with you. *This* is why you're here. An essential part of the prophecy....are you ready?'

Sure we weren't ready at all but we drank it anyway.

Fuck me.

## We don't have much time.

It wasn't long before the word got around about the Astra. Nobody doubted now that we were the Saviours. At first, they treated us with deference and respect, but soon they started asking questions. Nola told me not to give them too much hope, but don't be too negative either, and try not to be indifferent, but remain calm. In the end I didn't know what the fuck she wanted so I just told them the truth.

'We're lookin for these two burds we met in Galway....'

I was talking to a man called Séan in Paddy's. Old type. Big chest. Grey hair. Straight talker.

Joe was doing a crossword in the front bar. The rest of the place was mostly empty. There was still banners up from the party. A smell of someone making soup. Séan asked: 'Is it you that's from Ballinrobe?'

'Tis.'

'Is Paddy Donnellan still doin the taxi down there?'

'Doin a bit.'

'Sound man.'

'Don't know him too well myself.'

'I owe him a tenner for bringin me home one night.'

'Oh yeah?'

'I meant to call into him with it, and sure when I was puttin on my shoes I left the laces open and fell down the stairs. I was sick as a dog the same mornin. Woke up here not too long after.'

I was drinking Mi-wadi. Trying to keep things steady. Ice cubes rattled, cold when they touched my lips. Left the glass down with a light thud. Séan reached into his pocket. Took out a ten euro note, handed it to me. 'This is the same tenner anyway. You might give it to him if ya seen him again...?'

I took it. Crisp. Said: 'No problem, Séan.'

'Good man. I'll go again. I have to meet Johnny Kelly.'

'From Caherlistrane?'

'That's him, yeah. Do you know him?'

'By reputation only.'

'Oh shtop, he's worse than that.'

'Yeah?'

'Ya don't mess with Johnny.'

'Is it true he threw a Guard through the window of a pub one night?'

'That'd be him alright. G'luck.'

He left. Nola took his place. Long white dress. Pale. All grace. She asked: 'How's everything?'

'Good. How're you?'

'Nervous.'

'Car nearly ready?'

'Tonight, maybe. Tomorrow night, definitely.'

'Did you take something from Séan?'

'A tenner for Paddy Donnellan in Ballinrobe. If we make it back.'

'When.'

'What?'

'*When* you make it back.'

'Oh yeah.'

'Ye'll need music.'

'Tom said he'd sort it.'

'There'll be someone called Aquinas when you make it to the other side of the lake.'

'*Who?*'

'Aquinas.'

'Who's he?'

'He'll tell you how to get back to the roundabout.'

'Is he just waitin for us?'

'Yes.'

'For how long?'

'A thousand purgatorial years.'

She got sad when she said that. I asked: 'Is he someone important to you?'

'Just make sure you find him. He has to stay there til you do.'

'Tom mentioned....'

'I don't want to know what Tom mentioned...'

'Are you cryin?'

'Melissa's looking for you.'

'Where?'

'Down by the Waterfall.'

'Where's that?'

She told me.

It was a long walk through a wood. Thin path. Wooden gates. Sound of running water in the distance. Smell of dead leaves. The pour came from a considerable height, but a far cry from Niagara. She was sitting on a rock by a plunge pool near the bottom. Knees to her chin, elbows across them, unmoving. Another image I'd remember.

I sat beside her.

She knew I was there but didn't move, just stared at something on the ground. There was light tears falling from her soft brown eyes. After a while of listening to the splash and watching the white spit float, she said: 'I was praying for my boy.'

'Nola said you were lookin for me.'

'You can't fail, Jack.'

'I'll try not to.'

'No. Don't try. Just be sure you make it.'

She started crying more. Real heavy stuff. I didn't know what to do. She looked right at me. It went straight to my soul. I said: 'I promise I'll make it. Ok?'

She handed me a glass vial full of lime coloured liquid. 'This is it. It's ready.'

'The DMT?'

'Yes. It can be simply drank as it is.'

I took it. Put it in my pocket.

'Don't lose it.' She said.

She cried again for a long time. Lying against my chest. Sniffles. Vibrations. All that.

We left soon after. Held hands. She was quiet, but relaxed now. Our fingers were cold. Strong breeze. Clouds gathering. Getting ready to rain. She looked at the sky. Her voice full of pain. 'The clouds of torment are gathering. They know something is happening.'

'Tom said he'll have the car ready tomorrow night, maybe.'

'I feel so afraid.' Then she said something that struck a chord, scared me, made me realize I was going to lose her fairly soon. It went like this: 'We don't have much time.'

—

We walked back to *Paddy's* in silence. There was a bit of a crowd gathered when we landed. No seats left. People chatted excitedly. I asked: 'What's this?'

Nola was concerned. 'It's the storm. We think it's too dangerous to wait until tomorrow. You'll have to leave tonight.'

'I don't understand.'

'The prophecy says the dead will fight the odyssey before it even begins. They want to make the highway impassable. We think this might be the beginning. It's time to go.'

A shower of fear danced around my nerves.

Everyone in the place was staring at me. Melissa squeezed my hand, said: 'It's time, chico.'

Chris was in the corner, taking things from people. They were shaking his hand, kissing and hugging him. He looked uncomfortable. I said. 'What's Chris doin?'

Nola spoke. 'People are giving him things for their loved ones. The people you're going to meet along the way. Messages. Letters. Prayers.'

'Christ, Séan musta started a trend with that tenner.'

Things got rushed. My legs shook. Adrenaline kicking in. We don't have much time. Tom arrived, confident, said: 'She's good to go.'

'The car?'

'Yeah. The flux is ready in her and the radio's up and running.'

There was grease on his palm when we shook hands. 'What about the indicator?'

'She'll be sound. I threw on a piece from an oul tractor I had down the field there and she'll get ya by.'

'Your hair is wet.'

'It's startin to rain. It's the storm alright I'd say. How are ye fixed?'

'Just have to get going.'

'I'll pull her round the back for ye anyway.'

I looked around. Melissa was gone. A woman approached on the right with: 'Jack....?'

'How are ya?'

'Can you tell...'

It went on like that. People with messages for other people in Heaven, at home, Hell, everywhere. Parcels. Letters. Presents. Keepsakes.

In the end, Tom had to back the Astra to the door to fit everything in the boot. We even had to throw out a crate of *Bavaria* and we had an awful job to tell Johnny Kelly we couldn't fit a Hurley stick for his son. I thought he was going to hit me with it til Nola pulled him aside and told him to be quiet, and he listened to her, cos there was no other choice with Nola. Even for Johnny Kelly.

And then there was a roar of thunder. And a draft swept through the pub. And people began to get pale. And Greg came up and he shook my hand and he said: 'Don't fuck this up.'

And I told him I wouldn't and somewhere in the back; the first chords of *Heroes de Silencio* started to play. And it sailed around the room like a divine and powerful tremor and a woman in the corner began to cry.

And I got waves. And Johnny Kelly rose the Hurley stick to the ceiling and said he'd go outside and '...kill every one of the fuckin bastards...!'

And then Nola approached me with her sad eyes and they were sadder now and she said there was no more time to waste. And I still couldn't see Melissa. And then Tom stuck his head in the windy door and shouted: 'Will ye c'mon to fuck!'

Outside in the cold night, we pushed the car down the lawn and onto the stones in front of the water. It was like the final moments before a silver coffin is lowered into the ground. And then the water began to surge and big waves started crashing against each other. And Séan from Ballinrobe picked up a rock and threw it in to the lake and said: 'Be gone with ye cunts! Ye fuckin bastards go home...!'

And then Tom said we had to get going. Keep her steady. Just keep her steady. Don't hit fifth til you get up some speed and then don't stop for anyone or anything. Lightning now, red forks in the distance. Swirls of wind, whining like a fan belt about to break. Big splashes. A crescendo of chants from the crowd. And Johnny Kelly had to be held back by Joe from running into the lake with the Hurley stick.

And then I saw Melissa standing, still as stone, watching at the end of the crowd. I felt cold and scared and my courage melted. I walked towards her, and she backed away. And I walked more and yet she backed and Chris shouted: 'Jack!'

And then she walked over to me, and the wind tossed her hair. And we stood opposite each other and she took my hand in hers and she looked up at me with her sad brown eyes and said: 'I'll see you there.'

And then she turned away, and disappeared, and I got into the car and turned the ignition thinking: "...sweet fuckin Jesus my head is goin to melt."

Purring engine and *Heroes de Silencio* on the speakers now, haunting the car, but the chanting could still be heard outside, and the water roared, and in the rearview mirror was Nola staring, standing still, and somehow white, watching us getting ready to pull away.

And Chris said: 'Jack.' And I knew what he meant. And I put it in first. And the sky screamed and the rain belted against the windscreen and the red thunder scorched the water, and Johnny Kelly ran up to the window and he roared: 'Will ye drive on to fuck! Get the cunts will ye! Drive on...for fucks sake!!'

And he tried frantically to open the door but it was locked and Tom pulled him back and they both fell onto the stones and then I turned up the radio and accelerated.

# Let's talk about Melissa's kid.

*Psychoanalytic night and Dharmakaya light.*

WELL, after the wife left, there was nothing more to do. Nothing more cept go round the corner to the bald fella with the stall and all the answers. The fella they call "The Oracle". He was smoking when I arrived, and he asked me what I wanted to be, and I said a gambler. He said he'd heard that wasn't working out too well and maybe I should try something else. I asked him what, and he squinted his eyes and let his stomach think for a second, and somewhere in the far away grey day things were happening and people were dying, and losing their keys, and putting down dogs; and stuffing their dumb minds and bellies with food and needless worries. And here's me, on my last cent of Euro foolish money, down a back alley with a fat man they say can help when nobody else cares anymore.

And then he asked: 'Weren't you in rehab?'

I told him I was and he asked me how it went with the psychiatrists and I told him they were all amateurs. He asked if maybe I thought I could do better myself? And I said: 'Yeah, sure, I know plenty more about the human condition than most of them bald eggs in the Universities.'

And that's when he gave me my certificates, and told me to ride on into the psychoanalytic night and help the starving fools see the Dharmakaya light. He said he'd find me an office and I should stick these qualifications on the walls and no one would ask a damn thing about how I got them, or where they came from, cos everyone that walked through my door'd be so fucked up in the brain that I could tell them anything.

WELL, puddles splashed somewhere in the faraway street and heels clicked and women laughed, and men talked on phones and kids cried and birds squawked, and the sky was cracked blue, now, and all the rain seemed to dissipate somewhere into a distant blanket of ocean that went on forever and no one knew where, except all them scientists among which I could now sort of include myself in their number.

–

The office was small with two chairs and a coffee table and pictures of boats and horses and portraits of people probably long dead, and looking at us from the distant afterworld we were all doing so much to avoid.

I had my name on the door in the plated glass you see on the films, and when my first patient arrived, she woulda seen it right there in black bold lettering: **Jacky Denehan**. And she woulda felt safe, too, cos it's a strong name from a strong family, and here I am carrying on this proud tradition.

And when she sat down I fell in love as I do with all pretty women I meet for the first time. In she walked; all dolled up and looking for answers. And I could smell that old school Irish Catholic virtue that comes from these clean skin pretty blondes that walk our new secular streets. I could hear those moral marbles rattling round, behind her sea blue eyes, and I knew there was places she could never go, or things she could never do; and her virtues are all here to be seen and unsold, and for that she'll get points on the great big board of the sin free life. But then why was she here?

Her bag was filled with things I never understood, and her hair was washed, but untainted by modern chemicals and methods. Her face was pure and she had the vague smell of safe and unassuming soap that caused so many cogs to turn in a man's groin and he never knows why.

'I want to steal something.' She said.

'What is it?' I asked.

'A watch.'

'A watch?'

'Yes. It belonged to my husband's father. He died, then his wife took it, my mother in-law.'

'Sounds like you're lookin for a confession box, dear.'

'No!' She blurted, suddenly afraid. 'I'm looking for you.'

'What can *I* do to help?'

'Are you really a psychiatrist?'

'That's what it says on the door.'

'No it doesn't. It just says: **Jacky Denehan.**'

'Really? Oh. I'll change that to M.D....PhD...tomorrow.'

She blinked and asked: 'What does all that stand for?'

'Anythin but the Watch Police. Why do you want to steal it?'

'I was in love with my husband's father. We had an affair. He hated his wife. He wanted to be buried with the watch but...she took it from him when he died. Then she had it buried with *her*.'

'Why?'

'One last spite. She was a bitch, God forgive me.' Beat. 'I could never tell this to a priest.'

'When did he die?'

'Last year.'

'Sorry to hear that.'

'He suffered a lot.'

'Cancer?'

'How did you know?'

'What else kills people anymore?'

She thought about that. 'Anyway, I feel so guilty I want to dig her up and take the watch back. It's like a compulsion that won't leave me alone.'

'Do you have a JCB?'

'A...what sorry?'

'A JCB? Somethin to dig her up with.'

'Why would I want to do that?'

'You just said you did.'

'But I...didn't mean it.'

'Didn't you?'

'I did but...I wanted you to talk me out of it.'

'Why would I talk you out of it?'

'It's...wrong. Sacred ground can't be...'

'Can't be what? They do it every day with the Guards....'

'In Dublin maybe but...'

'What are your choices here? You knew the priest would say: "No." You can't talk to your husband about it and the woman's dead anyway. So fuck it. Get yourself a JCB and take the watch back. What's the problem? You'll have to hire a driver maybe but...'

'I...I don't know.'

There was silence for maybe a minute while she looked at the ground. Then she said: 'Now it doesn't seem so important anymore.'

'Did you love him?'

'With all my heart.'

'Why didn't you elope together?'

'It was impossible.'

'Why?'

'We're good people.'

'I think you just needed to tell someone about the affair.'

'Really?'

'Yeah. Do you feel relieved?'

'I do, actually.'

'Does the watch really matter now that you've told someone about your infidelity?'

'No. I don't know. I don't think so.' She looked inside herself, then went: 'No. It's gone. Digging her up seems ridiculous now.' Her face lit up. 'You're good.'

'Honest, maybe.'

'There's sin in your past though, I can tell.'

'It's illuminated by your purity. You're clean now. Confessed. Go home.'

'How much do I owe?'

'You're my first customer ever so I won't charge. Just tell your friends about me.'

'I will. The Oracle told me about you. That's how I knew you'd be here.'

She got up and walked to the door and then turned as she'd been trained to do so theatrically by so many overcooked films. 'The world needs more people like you.'

'Thanks.'

'God Bless.'

And she left and I lit a smoke and watched the water through the window. My chair creaked and lunch drew ever closer and the peptides in my stomach began to growl and the gulls were flying around and I felt the first sense of self-worth I'd had in a very long time and I thanked God for Oracles and then the wife rang and asked: 'Where the fuck are you?'

'Workin.'

'In the Casino? Where are you *now*? Vegas?!'

'I'm *workin!*'

'Since when?!'

'Since you kicked me out and I'm homeless and I need to get my shit together.'

'So what're you doin?'

'I'm a psychiatrist now.'

'A what?'

'Yeah.'

She laughed so loud and hearty I remembered why I'd fallen in love with her. 'And anyway, I don't go to Vegas. Never been and don't want to.'

'What do you mean?'

'You always think "Vegas! Vegas!" And I'm just not that kind of investor.'

'No, you're just a cunt. And you owe me money.'

'Why do you talk like that? Can the kids hear?'

'They're in school. You wasted so many years of my life.'

'They were good.'

'Some of them. But then you took all our savings and put them on a horse.'

'That horse was named after you.'

'I want my money, Jacky.'

'How much?'

'€300 a week.'

'No problem.'

'No problem?'

'I can make that in an hour at my new job.'

'Then get working or I'm sending my brother to see you.'

'The chef or the gangster?'

'The Chef.'

'Really?'

'Go fuck yourself.'

She hung up.

I needed to start charging. Or make money quick. Decided on the latter and went to the casino.

–

The place was the far side of town and owned by a dangerous man called Frank Rowland. On the way, I counted the cash The Oracle had lent me. (€500. Not too bad.)

Inside. It was dark and portentous. The roulette table sang when it saw me. I ordered a *Jack Daniels* with ice at the bar, and I drank it in one go and got excited when I heard the click of cards, and the voices of deadbeats and hustlers and dreamers; and the lullaby of endless money.

I sat into a "Texas Hold 'em: No Limit" table for €250 and bust out nearly everybody and came away with €3000 profit. Enough to pay Jane the wife with the nice laugh for a long time. The dealer gave me the chips and I walked to the cage and cashed it in. Old Gerry was working and he asked me all about life, and I told him good and all that, then I asked about Frank and he told me his daughter's missing and things were a bit tense. And then I left and walked into the afternoon light and bought a sandwich and ate it and went back to the office and waited for something to happen.

I had to go back, see, cos the dopamine had a grip on me and no matter what street I went down, it was leading me right back to the roulette table and the chance to put it all on red and double the winnings. And thick bubbles of adrenaline were running round my blood like bored inspiration, and I was depressed in the knowledge that the only way to feel truly alive and firmly in my station in this quiet, brief, and uneventful life, is to roll the ball and live in that short breath of demented hope, and watch the numbers crawl to a stop and announce that: "Yes. It's true. The whole of existence is rigged."

Oh, yes. Here we are in the office again and the peppers are oscillating somewhere in my duodenum and the diet coke is simmering away and there's smudges on the window and steps on the stairs and here comes my second client of the day and what now, I thought. What now.

—

The man's name was Bob and he was in trouble and his eyes were grey and sort of blue and he was about forty. His business was horseracing and there was a race coming up and he was compromised because he knew it was fixed and it was costing him sleep.

Through the window behind me I have to acknowledge the deep laughter of the demon as the money in my pocket danced and burned and screamed to be slapped on to a bookies counter without further delay. There was, however, more information to be gleaned, so I did what all the quacks in rehab did and I nodded my head in a way that said I understood, and also that he was invited to continue. He struggled for a second and looked around and rubbed his knees, and somewhere in the nowhere, horses were being prepared and people were making millions and the silence of the room was heavy like thick soup or tension or a submarine that was about to burst with pressure. (I am aware, dear Buddha, that this is all in my head and subjective reality divides our thinking into parts rather than *The One* but if this fella doesn't get to the point soon; I'll need to stab it out of him with the gold pen The Oracle gave me for luck.)

'The race is today.' He said.

The chairs hushed and the buses and cars outside seemed to pause in surprise and somewhere Chaos laughed and I cleared my throat.

'And what do you intend to do about it?' I asked.

'Tell the Guards.'

'The Guards? Hmm...what sort of people are we dealin with here?'

'Bad.'

'Criminals?'

'Corrupt....criminals I suppose. Yes.'

'Liable to hurt someone that got them in trouble?'

'Oh I don't know about that. It's just a scam.'

'Well then, why lose sleep over it?'

'It's wrong?'

'If it's so wrong then why leave it til the day of the race to decide? And then come to a psychiatrist?'

'I heard you're good.'

'You're my second client. And good at what?'

'Advice without the...condescension.'

'What's the name of the horse?'

'It's Cheltenham. Three o'clock. *Bodhisattva.*'

I took out The Oracle's pen. Went: 'How do you spell that?'

'Why?'

'So I can bet on the race.'

'Why would you want to do that?'

'*I* need the money. *You* need the money. The *Guards* don't need the money. Cop yourself on.'

'*That's* your advice?'

'I could tell you to go to the law but you haven't gone already so what's the point? Everyone now wants to be a Whistleblower but no one thinks about afterwards. Where are you goin to work? Who'll hire you? Who'd *want* to hire you?'

He thought about that and rubbed his nose and said: 'It's 20-1.'

'You're answerin your own questions here.'

'You think I should take advantage and bet on the race?'

'If that's what you think is wise.'

'What do *you* think?'

'I think goin to the Guards would be a mistake.'

'Me too. Now.' Beat. 'Thanks to you.'

I looked at my watch and Bob stood up and walked to the door and turned just like the lady before and said: 'Thanks.'

I nodded sagely and waited til he was safely down the stairs before making a run for the nearest bookies. There was one down the street, also owned by Frank Rowland, and for a second I hesitated. The man had killed people for less than winning too much of his money. Then I looked at my watch and saw that it was 2.58pm and there was simply no more time so I pushed open the delighted door and walked in with the calm collected assurance of a man who's simply about to clean the place out.

*Bodhisattva* was running alright and there was a smell of smoke and burnt coffee and scraps of dead dreams crumpled up on the carpet floor. High chairs and counter tops and glass walls and dolled up young ones working hard at taking bets on the cure for the three o'clock conundrum.

I laid everything in my pocket on *Bodhisattva* and as soon as he started running I knew what had happened.

How when I left the Casino and old Gerry asked me what I'm doing now and I told him I'm a psychiatrist and how at the corner of my eye I could see my next patient drinking *Ballygown* at the counter. And how no doubt Gerry had told his boss Frank that Jack had just cleaned a nice €3000 and maybe Ballygown Bob should go up and ask him for some psychiatric advice in his newfound role. And how convenient was it that one of Rowland's bookies just happened to be so close to my office door?

And now here's *Bodhisattva* on her three good legs and one bad and she's breathing like she's dying and all them other gems are flying on right ahead and in comes *Mount Karma* in first place followed by *Sour Dough* and in third place is the respected *Dense fog* and *my* horse, who knows? Could be running for years or all eternity cos I didn't wait. I just let the grip of the wet masochism break out in warm shivers around my turbulent skin and I walked down the street past bags of rubbish and rubbish bins and a line of taxis where all the drivers seemed to be looking at me and laughing.

—

Sleeping in the office was ok. There was one of them Freudian couches that was just long enough for my legs and my black shoes hung over the edge and reminded me of my foster father and I wanted to cry. I lit a smoke and let the tar and nico hit take hold and listened to the embers burn as I pulled long and heavy and wondered how long that sandwich would last before I really got hungry again and what then.

And what's a man to do on a Freudian couch, except think as he smokes, and so I played the two parts and let the conversation with myself roll on.

And I came to some conclusions about love and turns on the road and mad decisions that I took that could've made me millions but lost me everything. And them kids at home and how when they were born I was alive in the breath of creation and invincible in the love of fatherhood, and how all things had seemed possible and worth fighting for. And how that little girl of mine was going to change the world for sure and how all the sardonic smiles of the mystified nurses couldn't convince me otherwise. And how Jane and me shared those couple of moments that all life is about, and how she had sweaty hair, and that worn out look at having grown this beauty that was part of me, and part of her, and part of something else. A secret that we now knew, but never suspected, could be so sincere and beautiful, and how all the words in all the languages of the world couldn't possibly quantify what we were trying to say.

And then, years passed and moons rose and died in the light of bright and dark suns and time went by, rolling and crushing our days, like a heavy train over our love, and I gradually began to feel empty. Some tear in my gut opened up and things started leaking out and soon there was nothing left inside. And suddenly I was the Nowhereman.

No place in this world: And no confidence or control. I was left bereft of any choice in what happened to my family or my humble abode and it was dictated, dear sir, that you must struggle and scrape and eke out what you can til you're suddenly buried and that'll be that, there and then, thank you very much. Yes, I was the Nowhereman. I am the Nowhereman. The dramatic and melancholy and brainless boozer and gambler that provides nothing and is simply degenerate anti-matter, discarded on the rubbish heap of them that couldn't handle it, or fall for it; or deal with it. The thin film of deluded reality had been torn violently away; and now here I was looking at the bare bones of existence like a man witness to an x-ray of a terribly sick and terminally pointless world.

And I walk now in the shadow of taxi laughter and the dying strength of the blow that I always planned to strike. And how many stones have I kicked now in a way that says: 'I'll show them all?!' And even the stones don't believe me! And these days I'm simply worn down into meaninglessness, the delight of an inescapable current, like a drunk kicked out of a wedding and suddenly thrown on to a street in a strange town or city, with nothing only his immediate baggage of disgrace which shines from his clothes and stubble and demeanour and light wallet. And he thinks to himself: "Finally, now, it's done! There is simply nothing left to lose and I am free. Yet. Terribly lost and alone. I am invisible. See through. Transparent. I am a Nowhereman. Let me pick a direction and walk indifferently through the clamour with my secret. My freedom is intoxicating, yet impossible to explain to the commoner. Oh well, coins rattle in my pocket, the night breathes, anything could happen, I am alive after all. Finally delivered, finally born!"

—

What a fuckin couch? I thought as the cigarette burned to the butt and I didn't want to quench it cos it was my last one and what the fuck then. And then I slept and had dreams that were so bad that I woke up inside them and people told me it was ok, you were only dreaming, and I felt the sweet rush of relief and so much love and luckiness and gratitude for life, and then I woke up again for real and saw where I was, and I was hungry with no cigarettes and there was a big ball in my stomach burning like a globe, or an orb, or an ulcer, which I'm almost sure has been there most of my life except when I gambled and when my little girl was brought into the world.

I got up and looked out the window and watched the silent indigo dawn and there was nowhere to go. Absolutely nowhere to go. The Nowhereman again. And then I noticed a note had been slipped under the door in a brown envelope and I opened it up and there was a piece of paper that said:

*Have something I need you to do. Call down*
The Oracle.

And I couldn't understand why people needed to pretend they're in films all the time and why they couldn't've just knocked, and told me, and not slip this clandestine message on to my dark floor. And then maybe they *had* knocked and I'd been asleep in my hungry dreams.

*A wonderful, musical note of a name.*

I hadn't been able to pay The Oracle for the certifications but I told him he could ask me for a favour someday. And now here he was a day later asking me for a favour.

Walking to his place, there was music in my head in tandem with my heavy footsteps, and the rain, and the synchronised variety of life on the busy streets. And even how that beauty had to walk past like a chorus with her coffee, and the homeless montage of rattling change and the drifting montage of buses and gathering clouds and voices, so many voices. Their echoes bouncing off each other in this wild tomb, and cancelling each other out and crashing like cymbals, and nothing was allowed to be quiet; just energy transferring into things and back again, and swapping states through the infinite wind, and constants, and indeterminate secrets that dictate everything. It's so subtle you can't see it. Soon as you look it in the eye or try to understand it, it'll disappear into nowhere like a holographic ghost that'll evaporate into the air and become silence and distant whispers til you turn your attention to something else for long enough to let it come back and haunt your days again, like a cold shiver descending behind you; breathing the inexplicable on your neck. And no, you can't escape it, cos it inhabits everything. Even your drink and your thoughts, and the roulette ball singing round the wheel, and they're all in unison, and fixed in the beautiful current of what we call: Chaos.

The favour was to drive a young girl to rehab. What the fuck.

He said I knew where it was and it would help me remember things about my own addiction. I don't know what he was thinking cos before I even saw her I knew I was going to sleep with her. This is more of the cosmic union business and flicker of organised chaos that comes to a Nowhereman like me.

So she walked in with her jeans and her long hair and her big blue eyes and I couldn't figure out what the hell sorta rehab she could possibly need.

And then The Oracle lent us his car and we got going, and she chewed a juicy fruit and crossed her thin legs in the passenger seat. Her hair was brown and her earrings large and round and it was quiet out and sometime in February and things were starting to come alive in the world. Sort of.

I put it into fifth gear and let the needle hit sixty and then asked her: 'What are you goin in for?'

And she said 'Nothing.'

She wasn't going to rehab, that was just a term The Oracle had used because he wanted us to get to know each other. She was 23 and suicidal cos she felt there was no meaning to life; and this piqued something in the back of my brain and I stared at the white line on the road for a long time and then she said: 'He thinks you'd be a good person to talk to.'

So we went to her house and there was a mantelpiece with golden dust and it was old and there was a fireplace and the smell of ashes and I put on some flames and we sat facing each other by the warmth and her fingernails were painted purple and she wore cheap rings.

She asked: 'What'll we do?' And I shrugged and said we should probably get drunk cos Irish people only truly judge each other through the eyes of alcohol, and she liked that, and she procured a bottle of Gin and we drank it fairly fast but delayed the riding til we talked some more. And she told me things about her life, and her face was yellowish from the fire but her skin was perfect and sallow and things were quiet a little in my mind, and even my gnawing stomach had subdued its assault in the midst of my fascination.

And here comes her story and you'll think it's something about a tragedy or an event or incident, or even just a sheer life of monetary insulation, that left her unprepared for all the bricks and batterings that were to come her way.

But no: It was none of that. And as we drank the Gin and it scorched my throat in the self-harm sort of way that we all like it; I suddenly realised I was in love again for the second time in two days. But it wasn't like that Madonna surge for the holy lady with the watch. There was something here about her mind, that she was smarter than me, and always would be, and be smarter than everyone.

And she told me this plagued her and haunted her because of what she knew but couldn't describe. Because of the things she understood and the distance ahead that her young eyes could see, and how she was reluctant to enter the contract with life knowing that it was rigged and it was all a scam and that there were devious traps, neatly laid out, set out for her, all along the way.

And how because she was beautiful, she was destined to suffer and be sought after, and never truly be happy because the world would always demand that she search for more. And the same *more* would always disappoint and melt in her hands and amount to nothing but wasted years. She could never be a real person and would always appear to the world as a preconceived idea. Her beauty would be seen first. And her true self would never be known, or could be known, because anyone that was around her could never see beyond their own desires or dreams or addiction to her physical presence. *Who* she was would never be important or matter as much as *what* she was, or how she made people feel, and there was a person inside her that no one would ever know or could know, or would want to know. They only felt entitled to her because she was a commodity in a world where the strongest currency was to be desired, or to own that which is desired most, and she was pure gold, and represented all the derelict dreams come to life for all the losers that didn't know they were losers, just lived in the blind delusion that they were somehow in control, and everything was *theirs* because they deserved it. Even her.

And after I came, and she came, and we both lay by the warmth of the dying fire, there was serenity and it got dark outside except for the last pitch of sunlight that hung in the spring night like a fluorescent bulb going slowly dark; and there was noises of chaos in the house. Ordered and quiet chaos assembling itself. And it got darker and the energy from the fire relaxed and we lived and breathed and expired carbon dioxide and pleasure and then it got really dark and the trees rustled a little outside, and my brain was dull from the Gin, and she told me her name was Catherine. A powerful, strong river of a name. And were we not living here and now? And stealing a moment from the nihilist night and experiencing something that counted and was worth it even for the short duration of the dying embers and the lukewarm floor? And silence gathered as everything was settled and order was restored and we were chaos together.

–

Catherine was dressed when I woke up and before I saw her, or knew where I was, I felt there was something special about waking this morning. Some other motivation to be alive and to get up and face the world. An emotion I hadn't felt for a long time and had forgotten about until now. And when I opened my eyes she was standing over me and looking down and I said hello, and she smiled and said that The Oracle would probably want his car back. So I got up and drank the last drop of fiery Gin and she gave me a cigarette and I smoked it greedily and watched her walk around and arrange things. And the doors were old, and made of some empty material, like cardboard but stronger. And the handles had a silver look, and were stained.

The stairs had carpet on it, and the floor was a tile floor, and a thin corridor led to the damp kitchen. And that's where she put on the music and I walked along this sleepy hall and heard the beats of what she played and smelled the smoke of her cigarette and everything was cold and austere.

And there were wooden chairs in the kitchen, and her hair was down and long and brown. It was eight o'clock in the morning. And when the song was finished, I don't know what it was, I felt absolved and energised and cleansed and ready for some great tribulation. We packed up and got ready to leave, and the front door had broken glass, and a round brass knob, and she pulled it shut with a terribly loud bang. The day was breezy and seemed to ask us: 'What's the meaning of this?'

She huddled her thin coat into her sides as we walked to the car and I sat in and she took the passenger seat and there was a smell like sour milk and wet shoes or camping or something. I asked where she wanted to go and she said she didn't care. She felt better and she wanted to spend some more time with me and it began to rain. I turned on the wipers and drove out of her yard and into the main road and the traffic was quiet and we went to The Oracle and returned the wheels and then went for breakfast. She had toast and eggs and tea and I had the "Full Irish," and she asked about my family, and I told her it was a long story about how I was adopted but grew up ok. How my mother was a Peruvian junkie in Spain, and when she couldn't pay her debts, they threw me off a bridge. I was three years old and was saved from drowning by a local fisherman and eventually ended up getting adopted by a Spanish couple, but then they were killed on a holiday to Ireland when their rented Fiat Punto was hit by a Pat the Baker van. They had no immediate family, so the Irish Government sold me to an old rich couple with false teeth and liver spots and a brand new car that they rarely drove. They were from South Dublin and, after a while, somehow got the impression that I had gypsy blood. They couldn't get their money back because the transaction was illegal so they brought me to Coole Park, in Gort, for a picnic. There were trees and families and brown wooden benches all around. It was sunny, and quiet, and they'd even taken out the dusty Volvo for the occasion. And after some ham and cheese and bread with olive oil and garlic mayonnaise, they said they'd back in a few minutes and I never saw them again.

And then I told Catherine I didn't want to bother her with any more stories except that I always loved Jane the wife and thought we were connected til I came a Nowhereman, and she asked me what that was, and I told her and she laughed.

And people rushed by the window but no one seemed to notice us and suddenly I remembered I was supposed to be working as a psychiatrist and making money for my family so I told her I had to go.

Catherine. What a name.

I didn't have enough to pay the bill but she said *she'd* get it and I could pay her back after my next big win. I asked her what she did for a living and she told me she worked sometimes as a whore called Marilyn. That some of the other girls called themselves Marilyn too, and it's sort of a joke, like they're Marilyn Monroe, but they know deep down that they're really just whores, but they choose names because they can, because they're the ones that's really in control, and it can be good money, and in her case, she liked to do things that hurt because it made her feel alive. She was only truly *herself* when she was in pain. Emotionally, and sometimes physically.

And wind blew and cancer spread and someone won the lotto somewhere and someone else lit a cigarette and a fella at the next table talked loudly on the phone about something he kept saying wasn't his problem. And I got a rush of something strong for Catherine, and then I got afraid of what it was to be here with her, and also that I had never been unfaithful to Jane, and I wanted to get on the couch and bake for a while. That's all I knew for sure so when she came back after paying, I gave her a kiss goodbye and she said ok, and she'd see me around.

And when I walked away, down the street, I could've sworn I heard someone crying through an open window. A woman. Crying like she'd just heard bad news and no one was coming to help her. No one at all. And the whole lot was getting me down so I rushed on over to the office and let the doors close behind me with a relieved bang.

—

The echo of the woman's tears still haunted me on the couch but I'd forgotten precisely where she lived so my obligation to go back and do something Quixotic was gone. Thank fuck. The office was inexplicably warm and I think the landlord was one of these jobs with so many properties that he forgets about some of them. Or better yet, the manic type that disappears for weeks on end and doesn't look for the rent. I don't know why I thought this, it just seemed to make sense and I hoped it was true, cos I was broke in a way that was fairly unfixable and I had no more credit with The Oracle. And then I remembered that Ballygown Bob the bollox hadn't even paid me. I'd been so eager to get down to the bookies I'd forgotten to charge. And with Ballygown Bob came the inevitable thoughts of the Casino and then I got thinking about rehab. That road on the way to the big grey dome of infinite fear and wonder. The walls were white and the other patients were Nowheremen like me but they just didn't know. They had what the experts now call *conditions* or *compulsions* or *disorders*. And how old Joe the cardshark was hooked on his Prozac to keep him level and keep him thinking about anything else but them cards and those Kings and Aces on the river, or that bad beat he can never forget, or the big wins he tries every day to remember. Deep thoughts swirled and found credence and ate time and let me wonder bout those days of dark smoky truth and educated medical types in suits that wouldn't know the difference between a casino and a cowshed. But no, they said, we were all sick.

Even Jimmy Doran.

And Jimmy Doran liked the drink. Whisky of course. Jimmy was three years dry one day when his car broke down and he took to walking. And he was mad, too, because he'd paid a thousand for the car and then found out it had a bad engine. Then he spent another thousand tryna do it up and the new engine exploded too, so now he's two thousand down and still walking the roads tryna hitch a broke lift and put off all thoughts of killing mechanics and drinking his problems away.

And then he wants to piss.

So thing about Jimmy is that when he drank he used to hide bottles of *Powers* around the place. Here in the press. There in the bins. Over here behind a tree and some under stones in random fields, cos Jimmy never knew when his wife was going to go mad again, and kick him out, or take all his money or whatever the fuck.

So now he's walking down the road and he's annoyed about the car and he wants to take a piss so he jumps the wall. It's a three mile stretch between his car and the town and it's all punctuated with green wet grass and bored old wise trees and grey skies and cows. And Jimmy coulda jumped anywhere he liked. At any moment in all that road but here he jumps not thinking, and down he lands on top of an old stash of his whisky. There in the green growth and the grass, lies a small mountain of self-annihilation.

So he calmly takes his piss and gets to work on the bottles and wakes up in rehab fourteen weeks later and he can't remember a thing. Tell me now, Dear Buddha, that the brain doesn't know what it wants long before we do?

And Jimmy still wanted to drink, even on the day he left the celebrated treatment facility, so he hit the nearest pub and sculled whisky til his liver burst and now he's not with us anymore. And Jimmy was a Nowhereman like me but he didn't know it. And the pain brought him down to his final escape and maybe now he's free, in some stellar breakdown of his memories and molecules. And maybe he'll watch me some day watching the ball spin round the black and red table and he'll make me millions.

And then The Oracle rang and told me that Catherine had killed herself. And wasn't I a total fuck up? And this is not long before I ended up in the mental, and fucked Kohlia in the caretakers storeroom, and how I met God and found all about my mother, waiting for me in purgatory, cooking up some fancy DMT, and fuck me, wasn't that a shock?

Kohlia, a wonderful musical note of a name.

*John Hanover.*

*High walls of intense grapes.*

Woke up in the homeless shelter. Heart beating. Mouth dry. I've been sweating for hours. First thing I want is a strong can of cider. Got up and hit for the road.

The door was light and damp. Pulled it open. It's a bright evening. There's a cold chill but nothing pneumonic. Figure I have enough cash for three cans and a naggin of cheap vodka. Walked over to the off licence, the focus of the world getting smaller all the way. There's a smell of something like flowers and it makes me pure sick. I'm nearly there and a hand touches my arm. It gives me a supernatural fright. A soft voice says: 'Excuse me, are you John Hanover?'

Turned round. Black hair. Oil on canvas. I don't know where this is going, say: 'Why?'

'I want to talk to you'

'About what?'

'Not here. Let's go for a coffee.'

I said: 'Coffee? Like fuck.' And I walked inside.

The wine smiled when it saw me. High walls of intense grapes. The fella behind the counter said: 'Howya gettin on?'

I ignored him and found the *Linden Village*. I'd just picked up a few cans when she spoke again. 'Drinkin heavy?'

'Is it that obvious?'

'It won't help.'

'I don't care.'

'It'll be worse when you sober up.'

'*If* I sober up. I like your eyes.'

'You're flirtin with me?'

'Don't get carried away.'

I brushed passed her and towards the counter. Her small steps in the echo of mine. I asked for the naggin of vodka. Your man frowned and got it.

Then. Outside. She stood beside me. I was feeling more social, knowing I'd be drinking soon. Asked her: 'What do you want?'

'It's a long story.'

'What age are you?'
'Fourteen.'
'Christ.'
I walked away.

Later, she found me on the arch and brought me home. Austere bedroom. Candles in empty wine bottles, wax down the side. No radiators. Two bar heater that didn't work. Tiny cheap shoes on the floor. Empty cigarette boxes and an old worn brush. She had greasy hair and strong hands. A smell like dust and perfume and something from long ago that I can't remember. What was her name? Sarah-Jane. Sarah fuckin Jane. Her eyes are black. Her legs thin. I've been crashing here almost a month. Been fuckin her too. Now it's twilight through the window. Sweat and life and time passing. Dogs dying somewhere. Children starving. Bombs going off. Some guy hanging himself from a rafter, letting the rope kick in, feeling good. Cars pass and stars burst in the distant galaxy. Supernovas and heat and my empty wallet groans. Sun goes down, yellow dime on the Galway coast. Falls behind the sea like it's trying to hide. Then it's dark and it's all ok. Hanover time.

Decided I needed to make some money.

So I fucked her again and left.

She knew where I was going. Out to rob anything I could to keep me drinking. The cum still tickled as the rain fell and traffic past by and night is truly here. I ducked through the shadows of the streetlight. I am a shade or a flicker or someone you thought you heard behind you. Ask me how I felt. *How did you feel?* Fuckin invincible.

Later, esoteric wind and glasnost whiskey. Drinking by the grass and the homeless water. Letting the beats go beat and the music hum. A world of grey colour and no cloud or promise. Sarah-Jane arrives behind me and says: 'Hey...'

'Hey...'
'How'd you do?'
'Bout €650.'
'Sweet. Any Smartphones?'
'Any wha?'

'Never mind. Can I've a drink?'
'Yeah.'
Handed her the *Powers*. Pink painted nails. Small mouth. She took a long pull, said: 'I don't understand you. You're not of us.'
'Heh?'
'You're educated, come from some big fancy job...'
'That was all shite.'
'What happened?'
'I saved a fella from drownin....he was tryin to kill himself.'
'So?'
'So two days later he killed his mother with the leg of a chair.'
'Why?'
'I don't know.'
'You're fucked up over that?'
'Not really, no. But it went down well when I was lookin for Illness Benefit. *I* just can't stop drinkin.'
She looked at the water, said: 'There's a fella called Frank Rowland that runs the city.'
'So?'
'So he killed my sister.'
'How?'
'Cut her throat with a garden shears. Bottle-raped her first.'
'Why'd he do that?'
'It's the kinda thing he's into.'
'Why're you tellin *me*?'
'I want to hurt him.'
'How?'
'He owns the hotel you were supposed to work in. His daughter is fuckin one of the fellas that works there.'
'So what's the plan?'
'We need to help someone.'
'Who?'
'He's called Tycho.'
'I'm sorry about your sister...'
'You're not sorry. You couldn't give a fuck...'
'You're right. I don't. Tell me more about Tycho.'

Her phone rang. She picked it up. Frowned and answered with a confused: 'Hello?'

After some conversation, she hung up and said. 'He's at the house.'

He was in a Skoda. I sat in the front. Sarah-Jane in the back. Tycho was bald and big. I lit a smoke. Dragged hard. *Newstalk* on the radio. The engine purring. Then I said: 'Did you want somethin?'

'Did you work in that hotel, below?'

'I was supposed to. But it didn't work out.'

'Was there someone there ridin Frank Rowland's daughter?'

'Some prick called Chris. I'll give you his number if you promise to fuck him up.'

'Do you know where he lives?'

'I do. I followed him home one night. Just to see. He'll either go to her place, or his own. Keep an eye on him and *she'll* turn up eventually.'

'That should do the job, so.'

After, he said: 'You shouldn't be goin around ridin fourteen year olds.'

Sarah-Jane in the back, said: 'What the fuck's it to you?'

I said to Tycho: 'Keep that up and I'll hit you a box.'

'How'd you get my number anyway?' She asked.

He looked at her in the rearview and said: 'Sure everyone has *your* number.'

I said: 'We better go.'

Inside she said: 'Does that bother you?'

'As long as I don't catch somethin.'

'You won't. I'm safe.'

'Not with me.'

'You're special.'

'I am. Amn't I? Special fuckin Olympics.'

I looked around. Wondered how many others she'd had here. In this bed. She said: 'I never bring any of them home. It's mostly cars.'

'That's somethin at least.'

She was wearing a denim skirt and she dropped it and I dived in for more. Sure what the fuck did it matter now? A week later she told me she was pregnant.

Then I had a heart attack.

Three things happened when I got out of hospital.

Nikki Henson was missing.

I was awful fuckin depressed.

Tycho had killed Sarah-Jane.

—

In the cop station. You can see it, too. Pale walls and motor tax forms and the surreal light of the law. Shoes squeaking on the wet tiles from the rain outside. Thick bitch behind the counter. She pulled across the glass and said: 'Yeah?'

'I fucked a fourteen year old.'

She went for shock. Leaned over the counter and looked at my toes. Sat back down and said: 'Excuse me?'

It went on like that. The "Super" was upstairs. A fat man with a moustache. He scratched his stomach in the interrogation room. Things were silent. I kept playing with a hole in my pocket. Then he said: 'You *rode* her?'

'Yeah.'

'Ya sick bastard.'

'What's the problem?'

'If it wasn't for wanting Tycho more than you, I'd have your balls cut in two.'

'You would like fuck. You think about the likes of her every night.'

He eyed me up, then. Picked his nose, and asked: 'How'd you kill her?'

'Sarah-Jane? I didn't.'

'We're talkin in confidence here.'

'Shtill in all.'

'Shtop actin the cunt now.'

'I won't, no. I want to go dhrinkin and I'm doin ye a favour. Tellin ye why it happened.'

'I'll need to know the details if we're to frame Tycho. I don't care who did it as long as we can do *him*. What kinda knife was it?'

'You should know all this.'

'Tell us again.'

'You think it was *me*. And you think I'm makin the rest up.'

'Huh?'

'You're some fuckin bollox.'

I got up and left. He shouted after me. 'We can still do ya for rape.'

'Do, so.'

I was walking home. Missing Sarah-Jane. Missing the child. Lost as fuck and empty. Then Frank Rowland rang. 'Howya, John.' He said. 'Have you time for a chat?'

That's when I said "fuck it." and I threw myself over the Salmon Weir Bridge. Expected to hit the bottom with a splash and relieved suffocation but I didn't. There was a stone bench at the exact place where I jumped and I hit it with a savage thud and two Japanese tourists sat looking at me like I was mad. I expected them to take a picture but they didn't. They didn't even have cameras.

The blood rolled down over my eyes and then I went unconscious.

—

Woke up tied to a chair. Dave was standing over me. He offered me a Major. I took it and then he told me he worked for Frank Rowland and all he wanted was Nikki back. I told him about meeting Tycho in a Skoda. He asked me if I had the number of the car and I told him I did. Thing being, I had a photographic memory. What was I doing in the cop station? I told him about Sarah-Jane. How Tycho cut her up. He'd tried to rent her out for the night but she'd said: "No." On account of the child. I wanted the cops to get Tycho but they were no good. Then Dave told me thanks and said: 'I'd kill you stone dead but you seem to be doin a good enough job of that yourself.'

And he left.

# The Bambino Highway.

*A bnggy and some traffic cones and big stones.*

After we pulled away from *Paddy's*, I lit a smoke. It felt good, somehow like control. The nicotine pushed in, hit some nerves. Couldn't see the crowd in the rearview mirror. Couldn't see anything but nothing. *Opio* playing loud. Haunting the car.

Black and swishing water either side. Didn't know which direction we were going. I was sweating and shaking. Hands barely able to hold the wheel. Unsure of anything. Mighty fires in the distance. Whoosh. Blast. Napalm towers. Lovely.

And then a big lightning bolt, with perfect aim, smashed into the bonnet. Shook the whole car. I felt the electricity go through my veins. Like when I was a kid and the oul fella told me not to shove my finger into the where the light bulb goes, so I shoved my finger into where the light bulb goes.

All the electrics surged, the dash went apoplectic. The Astra died, regained, died, regained. I hit the accelerator and all I got was the smell of petrol. Chris said: 'Well that didn't take long.'

The ignition turned but it wouldn't bite. She spluttered a bit, coughed when the water got above the wheels, and then we sank.

It was like driving over a cliff. The bonnet went vertical, same as a plane doing a nosedive. Stomach doing somersaults. The seatbelt keeping us in place. I tried gearing down, to get some bite, but it was no good. We were total failures. Most of all I felt shame.

Three cans of *Bavaria* went flying against the windscreen.

Beer spilling everywhere.

The steering wheel wouldn't move.

The car went into a spin.

There was a smell like a slaughterhouse.

I got dizzy. Feeling sick. Rollercoaster job.

Hit the bottom and the lake invaded. Soon we were drenched. Water on our knees. Up to our elbows.

I thought about Melissa, her chest heaving on summer evenings, the pop sound as the cigarette left her mouth. Brown eyes playing Spanish memories.

Then I remembered the Aquaflux. Tom had said it was a button on top of the gearstick. I felt around with my thumb and there it was. Round and hard.

I could taste the lake now. It was like piss and copper.

I hit the Aquaflux and it put everything flying, like an atom bomb.

And we could see all around.

A wave of bodies were scattered along the lake's floor.

Bones. Decay. Skulls.

Arms and legs and heads all over the place. And a buggy and some traffic cones and big stones. And a few other broke down rusted cars that musta tried the same stunt before. We could see skeletons inside, scared shapes, their bony faces saying what we were thinking. It went like this: 'What the fuck'd we try driving over a lake for?!"

I tried the ignition and, fuckme, it started. There was a thump at the boot, like when you back into a telephone pole. We both turned. There was a quare looking bollox trying to break the back window. He was like a fired extra from *District 9*. Too ugly.

'Drive!' Shouted Chris.

And I did.

The ground was rough but the car held well. My hair was wet and my eyes stung. The cans bounced on the dash. I got up to fifth and we hit the speed of light. Made good ground and then the water came back. A roaring black lion. It came close but the Aquaflux kept it out, meant we could drive on the lake floor, like we were in a fishbowl. The sounds were muted and sonar. Things kept thumping off the windows. Hands. Eyeballs. Screeching heads, roaring mouths, and kicking hairy feet. Twas like a floating siege.

Chris said: 'There's a forcefield around us, breakin a path on through.'

'How do you know?!'

'Joe told me yesterday when I was in havin a pint.'

A few times we thought we saw people we knew. Chris reckoned he saw his father and I was even sure I saw Chaplain floating around at one stage. He didn't look too happy either.

The drift was endless. Wasn't sure if we'd ever get out. And if we did. What then? I said: 'How long did Joe say this forcefield lasts anyway?'

'A good while.'

'What the fuck does that mean?'

'It means enough to get us through, hopefully.'

'And what's the other side?'

'I dunno. Do you reckon them windows will hold?'

'I fuckin hope so. That last fella looked like Bigfoot.'

'Or the Alien off *Predator*.'

After a while, things evened out. We floated gradually to the top and soon we were driving over the surface again. The Aquaflux keeping us from sinking. The lake had calmed. Except for the occasional wall of fire and dodgy tornado, we could drive straight on.

Chris rooted around. 'Anyone for a can?'

Drank a stray *Bavaria*. A light appeared in the distance. Blue, like the colour of those electric traps for killing flies. The car was confident again, ready to tear up the water. It wanted action. The lightning subsided. The waves relaxed. It got brighter. I thought of them all back at *Paddy's*. If they'd survived. We turned on the heat. Our jeans got dry. A smell of tobacco and damp. The wipers still going. There was a mad chance we might survive.

—

We docked on a soggy marsh. The wheels caught, spun, then climbed. The road was short. Darkness, but not black. A kilometre later, a big green road sign that said: *The Fringe*

We drove on in silence for a while. The light in the distance got brighter. I sat back and lit another smoke. Nicotine in the air. It reminded me of childhood funerals. Car seats and Benson. Wet clay and ham sandwiches. I thought of Kohlia. Got a blast of sadness. Then I had an awful craving for the sharp tang of bad white wine.

*The Fringe* was a pub. We pulled in and got out and walked over. The crunch of black stones. A smell like burning animals. Sky like a black soul. The keys rattled in my pocket as the door fell closed behind us with a groan.

Big window. Arty chairs. Long counter to the right. Guy behind it. Tough edge. Tattoos. Peak cap. Ginger stubble. Gave us a look, didn't say anything, just got busy with something behind the till. Green walls. Poster of Bob Marley smoking a joint.

A blackboard with:
**Soup of the Day: Whisky.**

**Dirty Girl beer on special. $3.99.**

We ordered two of them. This kinda got him nervous. He took the glasses from the freezer, filled them. Landed them out. They spilled a bit at the sides. We took a belt. Tasted good, left them down with a thump. Then, hint of American accent, he asks: 'So who the fuck are you two guys?'

Chris went for casual with: 'Just passin through.'

He took up a towel, said: 'A: That's a stupid fucking answer. and B: It doesn't answer my question. You want me to repeat it?'

Chris asked: 'What's the problem?'

'The problem is, my friend, that I've been here for a thousand purgatorial years waiting for two guys of your description to walk in and order two of the worst pints of piss possible, and now that you're *here*, I'm thinking it's a fucking joke...'

I said: 'The Astra's outside.'

This knocked him a bit. He used all his willpower not to look out the window. I said: 'We met Nola. You must be Aquinas.'

He was suspicious, like he'd heard all this before and had been conned. He took a bottle of Poteen from the back shelf.

Filled three shots and said: 'My penance is this – No Poteen til the saviours come. When they do, we take a shot together. If you are who you say you are, then we're good. If not, then we all turn to dust. You wanna take the test? I've been here so fucking long I don't care anymore. Dust. Saviours. Drunk forever. I just don't give a fuck. Should I fill?'

I shrugged, said: 'Whatever.'

He filled. We drank. It was the real kick. Causes an emergency in the brain, flashing red lights, Chernobyl shtuff, could be a nuclear meltdown. Fuck the bad white wine. He stared at us, said: 'Fuck me, it's about time.'

He loosened up. Asked a bucket of questions. About *Paddy's*. Nola. The storm. He soaked it all in. Then he said: 'Let's roll.'

*Rolling.*

Aquinas was Canadian and in a terrible hurry. He led us through a myriad of tunnels til we got to a room with a door that said:

Access Level Four.
No Unauthorized Entry.

Walked down a loud old dusty stairs. Beer burps. Groggy. The Poteen starting to sing. Passed a line of barrels and boxes. There was a smell like Christmas wrapping and cellotape. He pressed a button on the wall. The cement opened up like a lift to a car park. We stood inside. Three buttons. He pressed the one for the basement. It was bright. Thin corridor, toward a steel walled room at the end. Lots of folders and a table in the middle. Bunker effect. It didn't smell like anything. Some scattered papers on the ground. Plastic chairs. Aquinas was about my height. Lots of energy. He looked around at the files. They were all in alphabetical. He found one that said: *Saviours.*

He left it on the table with: 'Bout time you fuckin showed up.'

'What's that supposed to mean?'

'Shut the fuck up and listen.'

'Where we goin?'

'I'll let you know when we get there.'

'What's the problem?'

'I think you might be too late.'

'For what?'

'To get you back...'

'To Galway?'

'That's the way it looks.' He said. 'Unless we can do something drastic.'

He took out a file and opened it. There were diagrams. He found one. It was similar to the one Melissa had shown me at her house.

That morning. Her nails. Her hair. *Opio.*

The diagram was conical. He pointed to the sharp part. 'That's the limbo you came from.'

Chris lit a smoke. Went: 'And?'

'We have to get you through this wide part here.'

'What's that?' I asked.

'It's the end. Or the beginning. It should lead to where you originally entered.'

'And what then?'

'Where's this car?'

We told him. He gathered up some papers. Maps. The bottle of Poteen. We all had another shot. The brain liked it a lot now, a big fan. Chris asked: 'Do you know anythin about Nikki? Or Dyane?'

Aquinas turned around. 'No.'

'Nothin?'

'Are you fucking deaf? I didn't write the prophecy, ok? Ring the publishing company if you got a problem.'

'Just askin.'

'I'm just telling.'

'Alright for you, your fuckin woman is nice and cosy way back over there.'

'Fuck you. If we weren't in a hurry right now, I'd break your crooked fucking teeth...'

Chris took offence with: 'Your fuckin hands'd break into pieces if you hit me, you cunt.'

'Wanna bet, you fuckin dickface? Maybe I shoulda left you back there to get chopped into sushi for the fuckin dead parade.'

'Fuck that. If Nikki's here, I want to know. I'm sicka fuckin around.'

'Then stop fucking around and hurry the fuck up!'

He walked out. I walked after him. Chris said: 'Fuck's sake.'

In the car. Aquinas took the passenger seat. Blue jeans. Brown shoes, went: 'I can't believe I'm in the Astra.'

He asked me more about Nola. How she looked. If she talked about him. He seemed disappointed when I told him she didn't tell me much. Then he took a long slug, like the memory hurt and he wanted to shoot it down.

Either side was black now and barren. The road was thin, only wide enough for one car. All the trees were dead and grey. Everything was ash. There were no stars in the sky. No moon. The lights were strong and led the way. Chris got stuck into the files in the back, reading everything using a torch. He looked up and asked: 'What did you mean when you said it might be too late?'

'It is. If God doesn't act fast. We need to get you back, through the point at which you entered, and we need him to open the portal for us at the exact moment....'

'From the mental home?'

Aquinas turned around and asked incredulous: 'From the *what?!*'

I told him.

He didn't say anything for a while. Then went. 'You mean he's *trapped* up there? In a straitjacket or something?'

'Yeah, I suppose...he's tryna tell them he's The Almighty... but they won't let him out.'

'And how's he supposed to escape?'

'That bit's not predicted I think. We need to get the car back and work it from there....'

'I thought the Astra was *stolen*, when he got down to Galway...?'

'That's probably the official version....'

'I didn't know he was in a lunatic asylum....' He took a shot of Poteen and said: 'Oh fuck! Now we're totally fucked....'

Aquinas started thinking hard, not saying much. I coulda done with a fix of fast pints. It was hard to know if it was night or day. An hour passed. I was suddenly tired. Went: 'Where are we goin?'

'It's an embassy... we're getting close to the outer boundaries. The embassy is the last place before you reach the end of Hell...'

Somewhere we could hear a slow rhythmic thumping, like a washing machine going around with a heavy load, thruummp.... thruummp....

Chris asked: 'What's that sound?'

'I don't know.' I said.

'Sounds like a marching army.' Said Aquinas. 'We don't have much time.' The words stung. I went. 'Then tell us bout this place we're goin.'

He didn't say anything, but we knew he was formulating an answer.

'How long will it take?' Asked Chris.

He looked at the maps. Used his thumb and a magnifying glass. Tutted to himself and squinted. 'About a week.'

'Drivin?!'

'Yeah. Unless this thing can do the speed of light?'

'It can.'

'That's *true*?'

'I'll fuckin show ya.'

'Well that'll make it about day then. Hit it.'

*Ocean Port.*

The car heaved and bumped. Sound of a solid engine. I drank more Poteen and liked it. Opened the window and there was a smell of rotten eggs, like someone had let off a stink bomb.

Aquinas was working on the map. I looked down and saw: *Ocean Port Hotel.*

Asked him if that's where we were going. He said it was. But we shouldn't sleep there. There was a hut, not far from here, if the map was correct. We could get a few hours there, then drive to the *Ocean Port.*

I asked him what was wrong with the place. He said he'd tell us later. Mr. Mystery. It was starting to annoy me. I looked out the window. *Dire Straits* playing now. The guitar sailed light on my blood, caressed it. At times, when the sky went bright with lightning, I thought I saw movement in the distance, like wild roaring animals running in our direction, but we were going too fast for them to catch us. Caught Aquinas looking out a couple of times too, but he never said anything.

Eyes were heavy when we arrived. Got out. There was a smell like a public toilet at a beach. I was thirsty with sore bones. Opened the boot in the hope of something to drink.

Wheeng.

Went through the gear from *Paddy's.* Ruffle. Rustle. There was only books and medals and other stuff people had asked us to bring. There was even a pair of Wellingtons. I was wondering where the fuck they'd come from when Chris came round and asked: 'What are y'after?'

'Water.'

'No go, I'd say. What else is in there?'

There were flasks, a spare wheel, motor oil, a can of WD40 and six eggs. Six fuckin eggs? I picked up a fishing rod. Long and bendy. Said: 'Maybe this'll keep the dead away?'

Found some sleeping bags from Mary Monaghan. Went through the rest, smoking, exhaling into the stagnant air. Chris found a torch from Paddy Farragher. A big square thing with a long life battery. The whole lot brought back memories. Melissa mostly. Stuff she told me about music and the soul. Stuff I didn't' get til now, til listening to *Dire Straits* in this daft nowhere.

After, we walked to the hut. Aquinas was there smoking. It was a damp, badly built structure. Two benches inside. Dank ground. A small table with half-burnt candles. Chris lit one of them with a lighter. Our shadows flickered. I lied on the cold floor. Got inside a blanket. Oppressive silence outside.

I asked Aquinas. 'What's goin to happen with you and Nola now?'

He bit his bottom nail. 'I don't know. See her, hopefully.'

'Then what?'

'Work it from there. Everyone needs to spend time in Hell and Purgatory now so we learn to appreciate God. It's ever since those fuckheads took the Astra for a joyride. I don't get back until I get you through....'

'And if you don't?'

'Doesn't matter then, cos Heaven won't exist anymore. Nothing will.'

'Will the dead really cause a war?'

'They don't need to now, if God's incarcerated. They just need to get the car and tear down the gates of Paradise from the inside. This is a total fuckbomb.'

The sleeping bag was warm. There was a long crack on the ceiling. I moved to get more comfortable. A pebble dug into the back of my head and I pushed it away. It was coarse and wet and felt like a splinter of coal. Every so often there was a whiff like urine. I closed my eyes and slept like fuck.

*Timebomb.*

The next day. On the road. The sky was a pale grey. It was like things were getting brighter as we got closer to the edge. There was rain like acid and the car started burning up inside. Temperature needle went all the way up to the last, and when the drops fell on the bonnet, they burned and sizzled. The accelerator down to the floor, even though we weren't going that fast. The steering was heavy and the wipers only worked every ten seconds so there was always a few bleak moments when we didn't know where we were going, or what we were going to hit. We bounced off potholes and skimmed off dead trees and somehow never got a puncture.

There were lights in the distance. I hit fifth, but she still struggled and surged. The wheels spun on the mucky road. *Dire Straits* was the only thing missing. Eventually we parked on a hill and there was some kinda town below. Shanty houses and the outlines of people walking slowly around. No, they weren't zombies. They were something else, sedated or empty or evacuated. Aquinas said: 'The embassy's the other side of that town.'

We lit smokes and waited for the car to cool down. We could see whores and junkies on the street and people in wheelchairs. The volcanic rain had stopped, thank fuck, and Aquinas said it'd be wiser to walk down cos if they saw the car we'd probably get torn apart. We let that hang, finished our smokes and got out. There was a squelch and squish with each step. I was nervous and wondering what the hell to expect. Noises got louder as we approached the street. Music like at a funfair. And lights and shouting. Houses with broken windows and loud screaming inside. Blood on the paths, thick stuff and fresh. Crying purplish babies left alone on the road. A ragged looking fella injecting something into his toe. There were women on the corner. One was awful tall in a red leather jacket and black leather skirt. Her hair was thin and long in a ponytail. Her eyes bulged out of her head. We could see the bones on her legs, and hands. Her jaws were sunk deep enough to fit a pool ball. She had only a few teeth left and loads of scars on her forehead. She stood with one knee bent, smoking a cigarette.

On the left, there was an alleyway with a rubbish skip and a gang of starved types scavenged for what was inside. They were arguing and shouting and pushing each other out of the way. Every so often one of them would pull up a body part. Like a head, or a leg, or a liver. There was something cooking in the distance, too. We walked towards it. There was a fella there with a frying pan over a flame. He was really getting into it, almost dancing. There were cages around him with barking dogs inside. They were rabid and mangy; drooling and yelping at everyone that walked past.

A fella ran up to us trying to scream. He didn't say anything. Just had his mouth open, making a sound like he was choking. He kept hanging on to Chris's elbow and rasping as loud as he could. 'He's got no tongue.' Said Aquinas.

There was a long queue at the head of the street. Fellas with ragged clothes and torn jeans and no shoes. They looked like the woman on the corner with thin bones and narrow jaws. Nobody really noticed us. We walked to the top and this is where we found the *Ocean Port Hotel*.

It was like an International Embassy. Where you went to sort your visa if your paperwork got mixed up. If there was a problem, you were held there til something happened. Aquinas said: 'Ok, we're going to have to act like we just died, and don't know where we're supposed to be going or whatever...'

Light wind. We walked through the crowd and into the lobby. There was more going on inside. People that looked confused. Lost. Some had brown envelopes in their hand. Everything seemed clouded in a hazy sort of blue. The windows of the place were grey. We walked right to the top of the queue. There was a machine spitting out tickets. Chris said it was like the dole office in Galway. Four options:

*1.New Claim*
*2.Returning with appropriate Paperwork.*
*3.Re-entering Hell.*
*4.Re-entering Heaven.*

A voice said: 'I've been here six years.'

We all looked around. It was a woman in a black dress. Her eyes were gaunt. She had a bag full of bureaucracy in her hand. Thin as a rake.

Chris said: 'Where's here?'

'You're on the borders of existence. When did you arrive?'

Her teeth were yellow and her tongue a bruised blue. I said: 'Just now.'

'Oh.' She said. 'God is dead you know?'

Aquinas said: 'Dead?'

'That's what they're saying...otherwise, why is Heaven closed?' There were people thrown on the ground behind her. Sorta stoned looking. Life sucked out of them. 'And why can't they decide who to let in and who to keep out?'

I looked her up and down. Red blotches on her face. Long black fingernails. No shoes and dirty feet. Behind her was a man sitting against the wall with his eyes closed, lids shut tight, like he was praying the world wouldn't be there when he opened them again. Aquinas went: 'You're here *six* years?'

She went. 'Far's I can tell, but there's no time here really. Sometimes I think it would be a pleasure to die and then I realize I've done that already and there's nothing left to do but wait.'

Chris asked: 'What number are you?'

She handed it to him.

*500,187.*

Shtop. He handed it back to her and looked at us and said. 'What now?'

Her name was Vera. She said: 'You can go back to the end of the queue.'

'We're sort of a special case.' Said Chris.

'Aren't we all?' Said Vera. 'Now wait til it's your turn.'

'Let's take a walk.' Said Aquinas.

It began to rain. Light drops, tame damp. Normal stuff. No acid. Reminded me of Galway. Dyane. The Spanish busker singing *Pink Floyd*. Mostly of a time gone by, a far cry from the last realm of Hell.

We walked on passed the line of the desperate dead and A4 Envelopes and paperwork. Some sat smoking against the flaking wall. Others were sprawled on the pavement, like they'd given up.

Chris asked: 'Did you notice anythin about the hotel, Jack?'

'Like what?'

'Like it's where we used to work.'

'Is it fuck?'

'Tis.'

Aquinas asked: 'Did it disappear back in Galway, too?'

'Yeah.'

'Well now you know why.'

We went to the car to make a plan.

*Fission.*

The portal was the other side of the hotel. There was no way to break through and God wasn't there to open it because of his awkward predicament. Eventually, Aquinas said: 'I'd hoped it wouldn't come to this.'

'To what?' Asked Chris.

He took out his bag, said: 'We're going to have to blow the whole fuckin thing up.'

'Why?'

'We'll cause a chain reaction. Split the nucleus of the portal and you can squeeze through, it's like a Time warp or an Event Horizon.'

'You'd need somethin nuclear for that.' Said Chris.

Aquinas took a box out of his bag, said: 'Here's one I made earlier.'

'What's that?' I asked him.

'It's like a tiny Nuclear Reactor – basically a box of enriched Uranium with a million volt charge.'

'Where'd you get that?'

'You sit around for a thousand Purgatorial years; you can pretty much do anything....'

It was about the size of a car battery with red and white wires at the side. There was a small timer on the front. He looked at it all proud, delighted with himself.

Chris said: 'That'll just kill everybody.'

'Not at the speed of light.'

'Why?'

'Cos Time is relative. While we're all out here burning at a relatively slow rate, you'll be both breezing through.'

'And it what? Tears a hole?'

'Yeah. Hopefully.'

'Hopefully?'

'I'm going to set it beside the hotel and hope the explosion forces the portal open, but you'll have to be fast. It's like opening and closing a window.'

'How does it work?' Asked Chris.

'It's an atomic explosion, how the fuck do you think? It blows everything to shit.'

'Yeah but...'

'I don't have time to give a science lecture, ok?' I'm going down there, and I'm gonna walk right up to the barrier and set this thing off, but before that...' He took a flare out of his bag. 'I'll release this flare. That's when you start driving. I'll time it for ten seconds after I give the signal. That's all you have. If you fuck it up, you'll burn like everyone else....'

'What about you?' I asked.

'I'll fry.'

'Heh?!'

'Yeah.'

'Sure that's shite talk.'

'It's necessary.'

'Necessary?' Said Chris. 'You'll be fuckin cooked.'

'A million volts of Uranium will do that, yeah.'

'And what about everyone down there?'

'If you get the car back to God, then it'll all be reversed. Everyone here'll be saved that's supposed to be saved.'

'Even you?'

'No. I'll be too close to the reaction. I'll die.'

'Aquinas. You can't do that.'

'I can and it's happening.'

'When?'

'Now.'

He opened the passenger door. I said: 'Just like that?'

'Admit it, you're relieved. You'll be going home.'

'What about Nola?'

'If you see her again...then it was worth it.'

And he walked off. Down the hill. Himself and his nuclear bag.

Jaysus.

Back to

# Dave

**And some**
*Imaginary butterflies in the corner.*

Kirby brought us downstairs. Hogan was in the car outside. The rain belted on. The night growled. Robin was worried. We sat in. I lit a major, let it belt the arteries. Hogan was quiet, looked at Robin's legs, then said: 'Tell them, Kirby.'

Kirby said: 'I went to the hotel. It's gone.'

'Gone where?' I asked.

*'Fisherman's Blues.'*

'When?'

'Last night.'

Robin said: *'Fisherman's Blues?'*

'Yeah.' Said Hogan.

Robin said: 'I thought that was a myth.'

'Not tonight.' Said Hogan. 'About ten years ago, God contacted me to tell me he was comin...I didn't hear anythin after that and assumed he'd changed his mind.'

I asked Kirby: 'What did you mean when you said Nikki was dead?'

Hogan said: 'Tycho killed her. He kidnapped her from her apartment and threw her off the top of a hotel about an hour ago.'

'How do you know?'

'It was on the news. We'll need to respond, Dave.'

'How'll we go about it?'

'I'll leave that to you.'

Kirby said: 'The portal opened on the Headford road not long after she disappeared. We figure the fella she was with went lookin for her.'

'How?'

'In involves an Opel Astra?'

He went on to tell me about God. Mary. The lot.

Christ.

After, I asked: 'You think Tycho's tryin to provoke a war with this Satanist shit?'

'He obviously knows God is....where he is, so yeah, Dave, I think he senses an opportunity...' He got mad, then: 'Either way, he just killed my daughter so who gives a fuck *why* he's doin it!'

'So what do we do?' Asked Kirby. 'Should we not bury Nikki or somethin...?'

'Tycho stole her body from the morgue....he let the news report her death and then he stole her back....'

'What the fuck's he want her body for?'

'He probably wants to skullfuck it durin a Black Mass.' Said Hogan.

Beat, then I asked: 'So what the fuck do we do?'

'We'll need to talk to God. Make a deal to reincarnate Nikki.'

'When?'

He looked at me. 'You busy right now?'

Kirby said he'd keep looking for Tycho. I told Robin to stay at home and lock the doors, then we drove to the hospital. Through Westside. Yellow lights in the dark rainy night. The nurse recognized Hogan. His mother had died there a few years back. Long story of schizophrenia. Had set herself on fire beside a teenager. Smoke inhalation.

'Hello?' Said the nurse, and squinted like she didn't know if I was a patient or a visitor.

'I'm lookin for God.'

'I see.'

'Is he there?'

I took out the gun. She played incontinent. 'Can you hang on a second?'

She tried to close the door but I hit her a box in the mouth. Walked down the corridor. The walls were a mix of pink and blue. It was quiet except for the blast of a radio somewhere. There was a fella rubbing his finger on the wall, making the figure eight. Orderlies chatted and jangled keys. Our shoes squeaked. There was a fella with his head against the ground muttering prayers. A woman with wild hair and no teeth. Doctors chatting by a desk. Something about cheap food in Spanish resorts. They sensed us coming and turned around.

The doctor was some kinda Pakie. He went for the hands out, "let's calm down" effect. I shot him in the mouth before he said a word. The nurses went cryogenic, hands to their mouth, etc.

'Where's God?' I asked.

That's when my brother-in law arrived. In again for something to do with gambling and suicide. 'Hey, Dave.'

'Do you know where he is?'

'Down here.'

We walked down. He made small talk along the way. How was I? And Hello Mr. Rowland, and how's *Bodhisattva* doing?

We got to the end of the corridor. There was a fella scratching his arse with a fork. Another trying to catch imaginary butterflies in the corner. A woman came up and asked me if I knew any O'Grady's from Bellmullet. I looked just like one of them. There was a pool table with no balls or cues. Cups left around a telly blaring with some kind of kids show. Jacky brought me over to a bed surrounded by a curtain. 'Over here.' He said.

And he pulled the curtain back.

*The Super's dealin' with it.*

Left the hospital after that. Hogan was pale, he said: 'What do you reckon?'

'We've fuck all choice. Do you want her back or not?'

'What the fuck do *you* think?'

'I better get to work so.'

'You better. Fast.'

He left.

Phone rang. It was Kirby. 'There's some fella at the station that knows where Tycho might be.'

'Can you be more specific?'

'No. His name's John Hamburg or somethin… And I can't be there. The Super's dealin with it.'

'The fat cunt?'

'Yeah.'

'Any sign of Nikki's body?'

'I'm lookin, I'm fuckin lookin. Some call's after comin in from Knocknacarra, I need to go and see what the story is…'

And he hung up.

*No arguments there.*

After meeting Hanover, I went to The Oracle for guns. He was up and said: 'Howya, Dave.' The man never slept as far as anyone knew. The light bounced off his bald head. What was I looking for? I was going to kill Tycho and all his crew. That was the deal with God. Tycho had been helping the dead. That was the whole angle. Kidnapping Nikki. Attacking Hogan. They were looking for the car and they'd almost found it, til it went to *Fisherman's Blues*. Now it was on the way back and we had to make sure it wasn't intercepted by donkeys. No arguments there.

Went for a Glock and an AK47. And some grenades just in case. Asked him if he'd heard about Nikki. He had. Asked him if he knew when the car was back and he said no, but the Ferryman might. Said sound and picked up my stuff and left.

Went over to the Ferryman. He was hacking the head off a fat fella in a suit. He sensed me coming, went: 'More already?'

'Not yet. I was in St. Mary's.'

'They're sayin God is in there.'

'How'd you know?'

'Whispers. Spend this much time around death and you hear things.' He stood up. 'I seen Nikki got thrown off the top of the Clybaun.'

'She did. God'll bring her back to life if we can find her body.'

'It's gone?'

'Yeah. Stolen from the morgue. I'll need to find it. Let me know if she comes your way.'

'Tycho has her.'

'I'm figurin that.'

'I'm fairly sure of it. Remember that tattoo you showed me?'

'Yeah. It was two hours ago. I'm not a fuckin goldfish.'

'It's Black Magic shit. Devil Worship. I was thinking more about it afterwards. They were recruitn in jail.'

'I know...you told me all this.'

'I'm just sayin… if they have Nikki's body, God knows what they're doin to her….'

'God hasn't a clue. I was talkin to him half an hour ago.'

'How is he?'

'Middlin. Worse if we don't get this car.'

'Are you still goin to kill Tycho?'

'I'll have to.'

'Well that's no harm.'

'I'll give you the twist.'

'I'll do it for free. Good thing the car's on the way back.'

'How do you know?'

He pointed. 'Look over there.'

There was lightning and storm clouds in the distance. 'That's the Headford Road roundabout. They'll be here tomorrow. I'd say they're after blowin the shite out of the portal tryin to get back…'

'I'll be waitin. Did you ever see the likes of it?'

'No.' He said. 'And I'm around a long time.'

I left. Some story. Only Nikki. Drove to the Headford road. The storm was getting worse alright. Had a night to wait. A whole night and a boot full of guns. Lit a major. Kirby rang again, said: 'I'm at Robin's.'

'And?'

'They got her.'

'Who?'

'Tycho's crew.'

A shiver of something lethal. 'Is she dead?'

'She's in pieces, Dave.'

I drove over. Kirby wasn't lying. She was on the bed and her stomach was cut open and there was blood everywhere. They'd taken her eyes too and probably fucked her. A card for *The Red Dragon* on the floor. Kirby said: 'I'm sorry.'

And he meant it.

## *Killin Tycho.*

Tycho wasn't that hard to find in the end. John Hanover gave me his car's registration and Kirby radioed all the Guards to keep an eye out for it.

It was spotted by a squad an hour later, outside an abandoned Warehouse in Westside. A regular place for junkies and deadbeats and fuck ups.

I got there around midnight. They were sitting on crates and playing cards. Bottles of beer left around, and cigarette smoke in the air. I opened with a grenade and that caused a good panic. Then there was all the usual firing and fuckin around til I killed every one of them except Tycho.

I tortured him til he told me where Nikki's body was. He was hard to break at first. The electrocution or the chainsaw didn't work. Pulled out a couple of teeth and chopped off a finger. He still wouldn't stir. So I hung him upside down and went to find his brother, Jesse. He was in *Freddie's* trying to drink a pint with his fucked up hands. He recognized me straight away and went to run but I caught him by the collar and pulled him over to the car.

Tycho stirred a bit when I brought him back. He said: 'What the fuck does my brother have to do with this?'

'Tell me where Nikki is.'

'Let him go first.'

'This is not a negotiation.'

I poured some battery acid into Jesse's left eye. He screamed a lot before going unconscious with the pain. Tycho broke after that and told me she was in the boot of the Skoda outside. Went to check. And there she was. All cold and beautiful. I picked her up and carried her to my Honda and put her in the back seat all nice and soft and gentle. A warm wind blew, something inside me tried to stir, and then it died and I went back inside.

There, Tycho said: 'It's too late, there's nothin you can do.'

'About what?'

'Her. The car. Anythin...I'm nothin compared to what's comin...'

'You weren't much in the first place.'

'Will you let my brother go at least?'

I thought about it and said: 'I tried that before. Didn't work out too well.'

'But I'll be gone if you kill me. And he's no threat to anyone on his own.'

'I'll let him go so.'

'Will ya?'

'Will I fuck.'

I found a long chain in the corner. Used for a crane or something. I wrapped it around Jesse's neck and hung him slowly off the rafters. Tycho screamed through the whole performance and it gave me great satisfaction. After, I took out the chainsaw and used it right this time.

*Chris and Jack's return through the roundabout.*

*Higher State of Consciousness.*

We backed back down the hill. Tried to find a plateau where we could gather up some speed. There was a hundred yard stretch leading into the far side of the town and there was a tasty bump at the end that could act like a ramp. We faced for that. Put on *Higher State of Consciousness* and waited for the flare.

Chris said: 'This is the besht yet.'

'What choice do we have?'

'Fuckin can't wait to get home.'

'Poor Aquinas.'

'Ah, I never liked him that much anyway...'

There was a sound like a distant gunshot. Chris pointed towards the hotel, said: 'Hang on, what's that?'

'Where?'

'In the sky.'

'You reckon it's the flare?'

'I think so.'

'What'll we do?'

'Drive!'

'I'm not sure if it's *it*. Sure it might be a bird.'

'Sure what fuckin birds around here?! Come on, we only have ten seconds!'

'Right, right.'

The song was just coming to that whistling bit at the end. Reached its peak as we hit the ramp. Next thing, there was a big blinding flash and the makings of a mushroom cloud and it got awful hot. The car spun, we could see everything and everyone. The junkies. The whores. The hotel. The sky. The ground. They were all either burnt or on fire. And then it got even hotter. The music getting louder. The car spinning faster. I looked over at Chris and his hair was starting to singe. There was a smell like a cat with a burnt tail. The steering wheel was too hot to hold. I had sharp pains in my teeth and gums. Are you afraid, Jack? Terrified, Frank, are you? Every second.

Then: Bang!

We were through.

Home.

I knew straight away because it was pissing rain and there was traffic all over the place.

*Fella drivin it looks constipated.*

Arrived back in the middle of the roundabout. Trying to get traction. Skidding like fuck. Everyone trying to give us advice by pointing, flashing lights, shouting shit out their windows. Fuckin clowns.

We ended up on Woodquay somehow. All we could see was wet sludge on the windscreen and the taillights of a Range Rover. We didn't know what to do. The trees were hanging over the road like depressed shadows and people rushed up and down the street with umbrellas and jackets and bags over their heads. Chris was staring straight ahead. His face was smudged a bit cartoony black. He said: 'We just about made it I'd say.'

'Just about. Good thing you spotted the flare.'

''Tis, or we'd be like a tin of Nagasaki fuckin beans now. I'm half barbecued as it is...so what do we do from here?'

'Go to the mental and drop off the car.'

'But how do we get in?'

'I don't know. Knock?'

'And tell them we're lookin for God?'

'We could ring?'

'And ask for God?'

'I don't know. Let's just go over there and hope for the best.'

'If we ever fuckin get there.'

Beat.

'Must be somethin on.'

'The apocalypse maybe.'

'Worse. The races.'

'Shite.' I rolled down my window. Got drenched. Rolled it back up. Drove on. The car purred. Things moved slightly forward, then stopped. Chris was looking in the rearview. 'Nice cars, them.' He said.

'Where?'

'Black Honda Civic behind us.'

'Your man drivin it looks constipated.'

'Jez, he does.' Then. 'Fuck this. Try the radio for traffic reports.'

I did. The weather was on. All about Galway. Floods over the prom. Roofs blown off. Hailstones the size of your fist. Wind coming in from the Atlantic that was going to knock down trees and crush houses.

'So what do you think happens when we drop off the car?' Asked Chris.

'We go asleep.'

'Yeah?'

'That's what Nola said.'

'And we wake up back at the flat?'

'Where did you last see Nikki?'

'Her place.'

'Well you wake up there. I'll wake up at *our* flat beside Dyane and this'll all be like it never happened.'

We moved another bit forward. Things seemed to clear. Turned out to be a murder scene. Cops all over the place. CSI shtuff. Someone had taken the head off a bald fella and stuffed it on the branch of a tree. Lots of spectators, pointing, taking pictures and videos.

We drove on. Up through Woodquay.

Your one Stella was smoking outside *McSwiggan's*. From the first night I got barred. I gave her a beep and a wave. Her face got all scrunched, like it said: 'Who's that fuckin wanker?

We got to Newcastle road, almost at the hospital.

'What do you reckon?' I asked.

'I might get a cup of tea in *Supermacs*.'

I parked up. He went in and came back and said: 'They're sayin there was war in Galway last night.'

'How d'ya mean?'

'Fella in there told me at the counter. Said it was Frank Rowland's gang against some other crew.'

'Lovely.'

'Place behind *Monroe's* blown up. Body parts floatin around the water in the docks and some young dealer killed in Knocknacarra.'

'We missed all the craic so.'

We drove over towards St. Mary's. Got there. Everyone was parked like a retard. Cars abandoned up on paths and in yellow boxes and fired in behind skips and generally in the way. Found a spot for the Astra in a place reserved for *Ambulances Only*. About to get out when there was a knock on the window. Some mental cunt in a long coat with a gun. Chris rolled down the glass and said: 'Yeah?'

'Howye, lads.' He said. 'I'm Dave.'

*Dave meets God.*

They gave me the DMT. I called Rowland and told him I had it, then I went inside and handed it to God. After, I went back to the Astra. The two fuckheads were still inside. I talked in the window of the clown driving. Said: 'God said to say he owes you a few favours.'

'Ok. Thanks, Dave.'

'Now fuck off. He needs the car.'

'Just like that?'

'It's the most painless way possible.'

They got out and wandered away. I drove the Astra to the front door and God emerged. Gave him the wheels and followed him to the Headford Road, just in case something stupid happened. He hit fifth on his first spin around and there was a big flash and then he was gone. Only the rain and the traffic and all the losers left.

I turned round and faced for Knocknacara. I'd asked him to bring Robin back too. Got to her place and knocked. She answered, didn't know anything bout being killed, just wondered if I'd sorted the thing for Hogan. Told her I had and left. Next, it was time to check on Nikki. God had said to leave her at her apartment and to call her landline when he was gone back. She answered with: 'Hey, Dave.'

I hung up and went to The Ferryman.

He said: 'You were busy.'

'I was.'

'Is Himself gone back?'

'Just.'

'Fair fucks.'

'I've the rest of Tycho's body in the back if you want him?'

'I'd relish it.'

*Chris and Jack*

*go home.*

We walked back. The weather relaxed. Sun even showed. People sitting outside coffee shops and smoking. An odd one even wore sunglasses. There was an air of relief, pressure release. The Spanish busker singing *Folsom Prison Blues*. He gave us a wave when we walked passed, but kept playing the song.

Got to the flat. It was awful empty. Few cans thrown around from the session we'd had the night before we left. Nothing else had changed much.

Chris said: 'I better go on to Nikki's.'

'Do.'

'Out of curiosity, do you understand much of what happened?'

'Fuck all.'

'Me neither.'

'I'll talk to you later.'

Then I was on my own. Went to the room. It was like a cell. Cold, and windy, and I was lonely for Dyane. I sat back in the bed and thought for a while. Then things went quiet. Really quiet. It started raining again outside. Nothing except the rain and the dark night coming down. I was afraid and excited at the same time. Thought about Melissa at the waterfall, and if she'd see her son again. And Kohlia and Jennings. And Nola and all of them in *Paddy's*. And would Dyane be there when I woke up? I didn't know, and if she was, what then. Fuck it, had a wank and fell into a slumber.

Ask me how I felt.

*How did you feel?*

Fucked.

—

Woke up and she was beside me. Newly born kitten. All that. Looked around. Everything seemed normal. Normal enough to think it was all a dream. I got up. Found my phone. Rang Chris.

He answered like this: 'Nikki's here beside me, not a bother on her.'

'That's the job. Dyane's here too.'

'Not too bad. I slept like fuck.'

'Me too. What now?'

'I suppose we better go to work.'

'In the hotel?'

'Yeah. We're on at two. Chaplin rang. Actin pure normal.'

'Sound sure, are you comin back here first?'

'I will. See you there.'

He hung up. I sat on the bed and thought for a few minutes. Dyane stirred beside me. There was movement in the kitchen. Like someone was trying to sneak in but made noise by accident. I got up and walked out. There was a fella standing there. He looked familiar, had the gimp of a drinker. Bad skin, bloodshot eyes, homeless hands. I said: 'What do you want?'

'You're not Chris?'

'No. I'm Jack. I work with him. Why?'

'Good.'

'Who are you?'

'John Hanover.'

'Oh. Is this about your job?'

'Yeah. Are you...the cunt that got it?'

'I am. Do you want it back?'

'No. I'm just really lonely. Can I stay here for a night or two?'

There was no doubt he was desperate.

'You can of course.' I said. 'Take the couch.'

He stared at if for a few seconds, seemed awful sad, then looked around the floor. 'Is that a bottle of *Powers* in the corner?'

It was. There from the session with the busker. A good drop left. I said: 'Tis. Do you want it?'

I walked over, picked it up and gave it to him. He drank it in seconds and went: 'That's better now.' He thought for a bit, looked at me and said: 'I had nowhere else to go. Sorry about this.'

'You're alright. It's the least I can do. Sorry about the thing with the job.'

'I'll get over it.'

He sat down. Stared straight ahead for a bit. Hands on his knees, smelling like mulled wine.

'What happened you, at all?' I said. 'They were sayin you were the best in the country at one stage.'

'I was. Not that it matters a fuck now.' He looked around. 'This is not a bad spot. I was ran from the homeless shelter down below.'

Dyane in the bed. Hanover wanting to talk shite. I was suddenly getting impatient. He got a bit sleepy. Like the drink was hitting him already. He started leaning to one side, slipping down the couch, drool out the side of his mouth. Eventually I went over and shoved him down slowly. Pulled his legs up from the ground so he was lying straight. After, I got a duvet from the back room and covered him with it. This seemed to give him great comfort, somewhere in his tormented dreams, being looked after like this. Then he was unconscious. Deep sleep. Heavy breathing. Sorta peaceful.

I went back into the room and Dyane was waking up. I lied down beside her and she stretched and put her hand around my neck and her breasts sank into my chest and her pale skin was all warmth and vulva and she said: 'I haven't woken up this happy in years.'

'Me neither.' I said. 'D'you want a cuppa tea?'

'Let's fuck first.'

'Sound,' says I.

How's that for Chaos?